The Misper

B E A ... T

The Misper

Published by The Conrad Press in the United Kingdom 2018

Tel: +44(0)1227 472 874
www.theconradpress.com
info@theconradpress.com

ISBN 978-1-911546-27-6

Typesetting and Cover Design by:
Charlotte Mouncey, www.bookstyle.co.uk

The Conrad Press logo was designed by Maria Priestley.

Printed and bound in Great Britain by Clays Ltd, St Ives plc

The Misper

1
Good cop, bad cop

Today's a new start.

At least, it's supposed to be all new, but people keep on blurting out the same old stuff. *Fresh page. Line-in-the-sand. Put-the-past-behind-you.* It would be a good sign if someone said just one thing I haven't heard before. Just one thing, you know? Surprise me.

It might be new, but it feels old. All schools smell the same, of sweat and Dettol and *don't-wanna-be-here.* The stench wafts out of the reception area. I'm hovering outside while little groups and cliques wander past me, shaking off the rain, talking and laughing and squealing and all of that. Some kids turn their heads to stare, but most of them don't even see me at all. I turn to see Mum give me the thumbs-up. She spent about half an hour fussing around me this morning, even straightening my frizzy hair and letting me use a dab of make-up to cover a zit.

Usually she'd say, 'It's only school, Anna, not a catwalk.' My heavy eyeliner and dark-painted nails are definitely off limits. Mum wants me to make a good impression. And she's going to stand there with that fixed smile, getting wetter and wetter, until I go inside, so I guess I'd better move. I raise my hand in something like a wave, hold my breath and follow some kids in through the toughened glass doors.

Over and over in my head, I'm thinking what I should tell anyone who asks about my last school or where I used to live. The thing *not* to say is that I'm trying to escape. Or that I'm running away from someone who isn't even around anymore.

I knew this girl, you see. A sort of a friend. No one thought she really mattered much, but that turned out to be a mistake. Because she blew a hole through my life – and the lives of everyone I knew.

Last November 3

It was just after four o'clock in the afternoon and it was pretty dark. There were smells of gunpowder in the air, because the kids had been setting off fireworks every day since the shops started selling them. Any day at school was bad enough without Zoe. And usually any day without Kerry was a good one. But everything had been off its head today, like a weird dream where everything you think you know is not quite right. The best parts of the day were when no one was talking to me at all. The worst parts were when people asked me questions. Three-thirty couldn't come quickly enough and I'd part-run, part-walked home so fast I was out of breath. And there was a police car outside my house.

I stopped dead and took some big mouthfuls of air. It tasted of fumes, fireworks and frost. My first thought was to turn and walk away again, in the opposite direction. I almost did it. But then I pictured the inside of the house: Mum putting out the best tea cups and searching the cupboard for some good biscuits for the police officers. She'd have that worry-frown on her forehead, so deep it hurt me to look at it. Every minute

6

waiting for me would make it worse. So I reached for my front door key. It slipped in my damp hand.

They were the same officers who came round yesterday… and someone else. The light-haired woman detective and the fat bloke who was her sidekick. They were just what you see in the films — good cop, bad cop. I knew how they worked. She tried to get me to tell her what happened, by pretending to be my friend. He tried to get me to tell him what happened, by pretending he already knew and that he could see right through me. They said, 'Hello again, Anna.' And I guessed there was no good news.

The woman cop gave me that sympathetic smile. The fat bloke already had my mum's china cup in his fat fist and was dunking a biscuit in his tea. And the circles round my mum's eyes looked so dark, you'd think she'd drawn them on. All these things made me feel guilty: her smile, his sneer, Mum's face. Even though I didn't actually do anything. No good telling that to the cops. After all, somebody did something to Kerry. Whatever it was.

I said there was someone else there, too, this time. Another woman, younger, with spiky hair the colour of apricots and a row of earrings in each lobe. She looked like a scarecrow that'd been pushed into a skirt suit from Oxfam. They introduced her as Jenny and they rattled on about psychology. It turned out my mum agreed this woman can talk to me. A nut doctor. Great.

'You've been running,' said the lady cop. I raised my eyes and I stopped myself from saying: 'Well done, Sherlock Holmes,' only because Mum was in the room. The friendly one was called Sandra. Her hair was in the sleekest bob you ever saw, like she ironed it along with her blinding-white shirts. I just shrugged. I didn't want to say anything more than I had to.

7

'Well. Get your breath back,' she went on. 'I thought you and I might go for a little walk and have a chat.'

'I don't want to.'

My mum said: 'Anna!' in a hiss. I didn't want to see her face so I just stared down at the tablecloth, the best green tablecloth. I stared until its pattern blurred.

'If I'd said that to a policeman when I was your age I'd have got a crack round the head,' said the fat one. He smiled to make it sound like a joke. 'We don't bite, pet. We just have to find out what happened to Kerry.'

I looked over to Sandra, who gave me a wink, as if we were somehow in this together. She stood up. 'Come on, we'll leave Rob to get even fatter on your mum's nice biscuits. Let's go out for a bit of air.'

Jenny stood up too. My mum gave me one of those tiny little digs in the back. It was like, Behave yourself. Don't make things worse.

'Nothing to worry about,' Sandra added.

It was darker and the pinch of cold in the air made my eyes water. The three of us walked down past the row of houses and I didn't have to be told which way to go. The Cut. Scene of the crime or scene of the whatever-it-was that really happened. Maybe.

'I guess you're having a tough time.' Sandra had a sigh in her voice.

I shrugged back. 'You guess right then. No wonder you're a copper.'

Silence. Then: 'Anna,' she said. 'I'm not having a go at you. I know it must be terrible for you. Don't treat me like an enemy. I just have to find out what happened. It's my job.'

8

'You're not doing it very well, then, are you?' I expected her to get angry, but she just laughed.

'You're right. I'm not, am I? But think about this. If you're having a tough time, how do you think it is for Kerry's mum? And the rest of her family?'

I kept my eyes down and under my feet the paving stones seemed to slide along of their own accord. When I first moved to our street I was a bit scared of Kerry's mum. She was really strict with Kerry and I could see why Kerry didn't argue back. She had black shiny hair, cut short and boxy like a man. She was – not fat, not really, but sort of square. You wouldn't rugby-tackle her 'cause you'd lose. I once heard my mum call her 'buxom' which I thought was a hilarious word. She didn't say it to her face, of course.

That morning, though, when I was about to go to school, Kerry's mum wandered out of her house, just wearing her dressing gown and slippers. Somehow in the space of two nights she'd turned into a different person. She didn't look square-shaped any more. Her skin kind of hung off her face. She started walking up and down and shouting for Kerry, until Kerry's dad came out, took her arm and walked her back inside. I hid behind the fence until her door closed.

We reached The Cut. The Cut is what it says it is, a little cinder path between Scrogg's Field and the other side of our housing estate. It's the sort of place parents tell their kids not to go on their own. They do go, of course, sometimes for a dare more than anything. No one used it when it rained because it was a total mud bath and you couldn't tell the wet soil from all the dog dirt.

There were stories about The Cut. They said a man kicked a dog in the head and left it to die in there. The older kids used

9

to tell the little ones that you could sometimes still hear the ghost-dog whining, at nights.

Sometimes Zoe and I used it as a quick way home from school. Not today, though, obviously. It had police tape around it and an officer in uniform standing at the entrance. Sandra nodded at him and he stood back to let her past.

She switched on a torch and beckoned me. It was the smell I noticed first. That mixture of earth and rotting leaves and dog wee, saturating the cold air. I shuddered. 'It stinks.'

'Places like these always stink,' Sandra said.

The frost had hardened the mud quite a bit, so walking was OK. Sandra swished through the leaves and branches, sharp and still icy-wet. She kept moving her torchlight around. 'OK, Anna. So you all came in here on Hallowe'en night?'

I'd already been dragged through this story, so many times since Sunday that I'd lost count. I couldn't decide if Sandra didn't listen properly or if she was trying to catch me out. There was only one thing we knew for sure. Here was the last place we saw Kerry.

'Hang on.' I stopped walking. 'Is Zoe doing this too? Have you even spoken to Zoe?'

I couldn't see Sandra's face but that Jenny woman was right beside me and she gave me an odd look, as if I'd said something really mad.

'What?' I said. A couple of seconds of silence. 'What?' I asked again.

Sandra gave a little sigh. 'Zoe is really not well today, Anna.'

'San.' Jenny reached across and pulled Sandra's sleeve. 'I can't believe Anna doesn't know yet. You should — we should tell her.'

My insides squirmed. 'Tell me what?'

Sandra turned to me and pressed her lips together for a moment. It was a long moment. 'Zoe is in hospital, Anna. We're not sure... They're doing all they can.'

I wrapped my arms around myself to stop myself shaking. It was so cold. My teeth started to rattle and I couldn't stop them. My eyes blurred and I couldn't see. It was so very dark.

2
Zoe. And Kerry

This is how it started. I only came to live near Zoe — and Kerry — when Mum and Dad split up. Mum said she couldn't afford to keep running the car so she needed to be just a bus ride away from work. And there was a school I could walk to, one that even got better exam results than my old one, so it all made sense. To them, anyway. Not to me. But then, nothing that happened round the time of their divorce made any sense to me.

I had friends at my last school, but only sort-of. I wasn't a total no-mates, but I wasn't part of the in-crowd either. I spent my time circling the outside edges of one group or another. Sometimes I got asked along to things and sometimes I didn't and there seemed to be no particular logic behind it. I often thought that, to be honest, it might be better if no one ever spoke to me. At least then I wouldn't get to hear about all the things I missed. All I really wanted was a best mate, but somehow they were all taken.

When I left, the class made me a great big card and it said things like 'Anna, we love you, we will really really miss you xxx.' This was from girls who'd hardly glanced my way in three years. My mum went a bit teary-eyed when she read all the messages and said she was sorry to be taking me away from so many friends. I shook my head and said it didn't matter, because it really didn't. Not that.

I moved away from Dad and in with just Mum, in a tiny little box of a place. Mum kept saying it was just right for her to manage and the rent wasn't bad and that it would all work out somehow. She was so wrong.

I met Zoe on my first day. It was May, which is a rubbish time to start a new school. The school secretary showed me to my new class and the teacher said my name while I stood there like an idiot beside her desk. I looked at the rest of the class and their blank faces.

'I think,' said Mrs Bennett in an overly-bright tone of voice, like someone who's just had a fantastic idea, 'I think I will sit you next to Zoe Sawyer.' I followed her gaze to the back corner of the classroom and the only spare desk. Next to it was the girl who must be Zoe. She was doodling and didn't even look up.

'Zoe.' Mrs Bennett raised her voice as I made my way down the aisle towards the empty seat.

'Hi,' I said, scraping back the chair. My voice came out in an embarrassing squeak. Zoe lifted her head. She had a long curtain of straight, milky-brown hair. Her skin was the palest and smoothest I'd ever seen, like paper. Her nails were painted black with scarlet tips.

'Zoe, I want you to look after Anna and show her where things are and where the lessons all take place. And make sure she settles in.' I could tell Mrs Bennett was already wondering if she'd made the right decision.

Zoe hardly said anything to me that first morning, apart from telling me where to find each room and adding, 'Enjoy,' in a bored monotone each time. At break time, I hoped we could sit and chat. But she opened a sketch book and started drawing.

Three girls strolled up to me, smelling of their boyfriends' or brothers' cheap body sprays. 'Wow, you really got the short straw,' one of them said. 'You can come round with us instead if you want.'

I glanced back at Zoe's black and red nails and the amazing manga-style drawings she was doing, all out of her own head. And back up at the three girls with their identical blonde haircuts and their matching label bags.

'I'm fine,' I said. 'Thanks.'

The others shrugged and turned away. I didn't catch what they said to each other, but after a few seconds the sudden sound of their laughter sounded like glass being smashed.

Zoe carried on scribbling and still didn't look up.

'You didn't have to do that,' she said, after a few minutes. 'Don't expect me to be grateful.'

'I don't,' I said, but when I thought about it, that wasn't true. I had some Disney-fied idea in my head that I'd just stuck up for her and so we'd suddenly become best friends.

I watched the sort of sketches Zoe drew on her book and I made a note, in my head, of some of the little things about her. She liked drawing the same sorts of things, again and again: skulls with spiders coming out of their eyes and witchy-looking girls with clothes that looked like cobwebs. Knives with jewelled handles and snake-like creatures with bloodied fangs. She was just doing them with a cheap ballpoint, but they nearly leaped out of the page, they were so real-looking. When she showed me where the girls' toilets were, she brushed her satiny hair in front of the mirror and tipped some strong-smelling, herby scent out of a tiny bottle onto her wrists. It wasn't anything I'd seen or smelled in Boots. When she got changed for gym she did it really quickly and modestly, like you might wriggle into a swimsuit behind a towel on a busy beach. She had bruises on her back. Blink and you'd miss them, she was so fast, but I didn't blink.

It turned out she lived a couple of streets away from my new house, but she didn't seem keen on walking home with me.

'I take it you can find your own way home?' she said. 'Don't need me to show you that?'

'Well, no, but I thought –'

'See you tomorrow then.' She strode off in the opposite direction, leaving me breathing in the last of her scent.

When I walked into the house, it was the first question Mum asked. 'Was there anyone nice to be friends with?'

I sighed. 'Maybe.'

'Come on, then, Anna. I've been worrying about you all day.'

'No, you haven't, Mum, you've been selling houses.'

Mum clicked the kettle on. 'Hardly. No one's buying houses round here at the moment. They're not even looking in the estate agents' windows. Anyway, I can worry about you at the same time.'

So just to shut her up, I told her a bit about Zoe. I didn't say she'd hardly spoken to me and that she only showed me round because she had to. But I mentioned that she lived nearby. Mistake.

'That's great! Why don't you ask her round at the weekend? She can come for tea or – or – a sleepover, if you like.'

'Mum, I'm not ten any more. I'm fourteen. I'm not asking someone round for tea or a sleepover.'

Mum blinked. 'No.' Then she laughed at herself. 'Sorry.'

My insides went hot. I put my arms around her. 'No, I'm sorry. School was fine. Take me off your worry list. I'll be all right.'

On Saturday morning, Mum had to work, so I took the bus with her into the city centre and promised to meet her for lunch. Then I sought out a shop called Dead Bouquet that I'd found by searching online. It was on a little side street off the main shopping mall and clustered around its doorway were bunches of kids, all with the most amazing clothes and hair. It was like a costume party, though I'm glad I never said that to any of them. I felt so boring and high-street that I almost turned and ran. At the same time, I felt kind of invisible, without the black, purple or red clothes, eyeliners and gelled-up hair style. But I made myself go inside.

It was a tiny shop, down a few steps, dark and smelling strongly of some kind of earthy incense. There was loud music playing that I didn't recognise and it was hard to get to anything because even a handful of people made the shop crowded. I could see the kind of things that I reckoned Zoe would love: candles that looked like skulls, racks of dark, theatrical clothes, tarot cards, heavy silver jewellery shaped like crosses and daggers.

I wasn't entirely sure why I was here.

I fingered a fat notebook, the cover embossed with a design of the kind of weeping-lady statues you find in graveyards, all grey except for the red of the roses at her feet. The inside pages were plain, so Zoe could use it as a sketch book, I thought. It was ten pounds, which felt crazy for a plain notebook, but I had enough money with me and without really thinking too hard I took it up to the till. I could barely find the space to put the book down because the counter was cluttered with lit candles in glass jars, their flames wavering at every movement, baskets of knotted-up jewellery and messed-up piles of leaflets and flyers.

'I like your book,' said a voice behind me and I turned to see Zoe.

My insides gave a little flip. 'Glad you said that. It's for you.' I held it out to her and hoped I wasn't blushing.

She didn't take it. 'What for?'

'I thought you could draw in it.'

'I can see what to do with it. I meant, why are you giving it to me?'

I felt my face grow hotter. 'It's – it's to say thank you for looking after me this week. I know you didn't want to. I suppose I was a complete pain in the neck.'

She thought about it. 'No, you weren't. I kind of like you. If I didn't, I'd've sent you into the boys' changing room and left you there.'

'Right. Thanks for not doing that.' I held out the notebook again and this time she took it.

'I didn't have you down as a goth,' she said, looking at my chain store jeans and my pink hoody, which felt over-bright and completely unsuitable, like I'd arrived at a funeral wearing a clown suit.

'I – I've only just found this shop,' I said, as if that was an explanation. 'I love the stuff, though.'

'Want to get a drink?'

I found myself following her out into the bright morning, blinking in the faint sunshine and the breeze, and strolling towards a little cafe next to the art gallery. The scent of incense was still clinging to our clothes.

Zoe ordered a green tea with peppermint, so I did, too. I paid with the last of my money. She looked even more striking out of school. She had dark eyeliner that made her pale eyes look like pearls and she wore deep, deep red lipstick. Her hair was in two heavy plaits. Under her coat she was wearing a blood-red velvet T-shirt that I longed to stroke.

I told her I'd been reading *Dracula* and how much I loved it. We talked about it and then about Mary Shelley and she mentioned some books I'd never heard of. Then I burbled on for a bit about my mum and dad. Zoe told me she just lived with her mum too.

'Do you see your dad much?' I asked.

'Hardly, he's dead,' she said.

I put my face in my hands. 'I'm sorry.'

Zoe gave a little pout. 'It's fine, I never knew him. I just wish it'd been my mum who died instead. He can't have been any worse than she is.'

I stared at her. How do you answer that? 'That's a pretty drastic thing to say. What's the problem?'

Zoe shrugged and clinked her spoon around inside her mug. 'We just don't get on.'

I waited, but she didn't say any more.

After that, we started hanging around together, at school and at home. I reckon Mum was a bit put off at first by Zoe's clothes and make-up, but she was cool about it, even when I started trying to dress the same way.

'Your grandma was really strict about clothes when I was your age,' Mum told me. 'I was dying to spike up my hair and wear the sort of things my friends had, but she wouldn't let me. I always swore I wouldn't be the same. It's not worth us fighting over something as daft as clothes.'

Dad wasn't quite as cool, though. He would come to see me at the weekends and he got a bit moody when I would rather be with Zoe. In some ways, I wondered if it would be easier if he didn't come at all. It was all so weird. He rang the doorbell like a visitor and stood on the step rather than coming inside. If he did pop in for any reason, he'd just have to make a tiny little comment and Mum would go up like a nuclear mushroom cloud. They'd start screaming at each other, while I stood there as if I was invisible. I sometimes thought it wasn't worth the hassle.

Plus, I was pretty angry with him myself, because he was living with some new woman called Ellie who I refused to go and meet. Even if I wanted to — and I definitely didn't — I reckoned it would hurt Mum if I hung out with this Ellie, like she was just some normal person instead of the witch who broke up our family. I would find myself starting a row with Dad about nothing and I didn't quite know why I'd done it. So all in all, it was best when I went out with Zoe instead of my dad.

I haven't said much properly about Kerry, and it's time I did. I'm going to say what no one says about Kerry any more. She was a total pain in the butt. There are good reasons why no one says this about her now, but it was true. Even when I made my mind up to be nicer to her, she didn't make it easy. Most of the time, she was the last person Zoe and I wanted to see.

The whole Kerry thing was all my fault, really, right from the start. Zoe and me got pretty close, after a while. That was just as well, because being goth meant that most of the other girls treated us like something they trod on. Maxine and her gang of hanger-ons were the worst. We were their new target for snipey comments and insults. But Zoe gave off attitude like some kind of force field. When we were together, no one really messed with us.

It all started on this one day when Zoe was off school. The teacher said she had a stomach bug, but I'd noticed Zoe would take the odd mystery day off and she would never tell me much about it, even if I asked. If there were fresh bruises, she wouldn't be persuaded to say anything about them.

So I was on my own. We were being sent out on what they called a cross-country run, although there was no countryside for miles. And we had to go in pairs. I didn't want to be caught on my own out of school by any of the other girls and get beaten up or pushed into a skip – that did happen from time to time. And I knew that Kerry was the only other one in the class who would have no partner. She didn't have anyone to hang about with at all. She spent her break times pestering the teachers and helping them tidy classrooms and all that little-kid stuff. I'd thought at first she had some kind of learning problems, but that didn't seem to be true, because she got great marks in things like maths and science. She just wasn't someone you wanted to be seen with. I'd mentioned it before, because I felt a bit sorry for her, but Zoe said she was most definitely not our problem.

So – stupid, stupid me! – I wandered up to Kerry and asked if she'd partner me for the cross-country lesson. She looked like I'd just given her a hundred quid or something.

She couldn't have been more different to Zoe. Or me, for that matter. Kerry was a head taller than either of us and a bit plump, with a haircut that looked like her mum did it with a pair of blunt scissors. And she had a loud voice and an even louder laugh that made me want to cringe. I tried to jog beside her and keep a bit of a distance, at the same time. Neither of us were sporty types, so soon everyone else went past us. One or two girls made some comments about nerds and loonies and all the usual rubbish. One of them pelted some chewed-up gum at us. But I had some kind of a 'Look after Kerry' head on that day, so I swore right back at them and gave them the finger.

We went towards the little row of shops near the school and Kerry offered to go to the bakers and get us something to eat.

'You've got money?' I asked. We weren't supposed to take money out with us, because we weren't supposed to spend our PE lessons in the shops.

Kerry gave me a big grin and pulled out a purse she was wearing on a cord round her neck.

I laughed. 'I haven't worn one of those since primary school.'

Kerry pushed the purse back down her gym shirt. 'I have to,' she said. 'Where ever else I put my money, someone finds it and takes it.'

'Just keep it in your bag,' I suggested.

Kerry shrugged. 'People take things out of my bag, all the time.'

'Right.' I couldn't think of anything else to say, because I knew what she meant. Some of those girls would grab your bag, pull things out of it right in front of you and then deny it to your face. I'd seen Maxine empty Kerry's books out all over the floor and stamp on them, just because she felt like it. No one ever stopped her.

I could smell the bready, meaty scents from the baker's now and my stomach growled. As we walked in from the grey, cool morning, blowing on our fingers, the shop was warm and steamy. There was a young lad behind the counter who I'd noticed before. Black hair and a crinkly sort of a smile.

'Hiya,' he said, looking at Kerry like he knew her. 'What can I get you?'

'Two sausage rolls and two cups of soup.'

I looked from one to the other.

'Oh,' Kerry said. 'This is my brother, Luke. This is Anna. She hasn't been at our school very long.'

'Hi.' I turned away to look at the fridge full of cakes, because I could feel my face warming up. He was kind of good-looking. On the way out, Luke grinned. This time I was sure it was meant for me and not for his sister.

We took the steaming cardboard cups of tomato soup and the oily packets of sausage rolls and we started our slow stroll back towards school. I began quizzing Kerry about Luke. He was seventeen and at the local Further Education college, but he worked part-time at the baker's. When I pressed her, Kerry said he didn't have a girlfriend right now.

'He seems very –' I hesitated. 'Nice.' Most girls would immediately start teasing me, but not Kerry. 'He doesn't really look like you, though, does he?'

Kerry shook her head. She was wolfing the sausage roll and making a bit of a noise as she ate. I tried not to cringe. 'He's only my half-brother really,' she said. 'My dad was married before.'

'Right.' For a horrible moment, I thought about my own dad and his girlfriend. Half-brothers or sisters? I pushed that thought away. 'That must be awkward.'

Kerry shook her head. She had flaky pastry crumbs on her mouth and I wiped my own lips with a tissue, hoping she would do the same. She didn't notice. 'No, it's really fine. Luke's my best friend.' She crumpled the greasy paper bag and threw it in a litter bin. 'I don't really have any others.'

Again, I didn't know what to say. Kerry finally swiped her mouth with the side of her hand, with almost no effect on the crumbs, and linked arms with me. 'Thanks for being kind to me,' she said, making me wince a bit inside.

I put up with her arm in mine for a few minutes then wriggled away, pretending to do something to my shoe laces. I didn't want to think too hard about what it must be like to be Kerry.

I felt quite pleased with myself afterwards, because I thought I'd done a good-deed-for-the-day. That should've been the end of it. Trouble was, the next morning Kerry bounced up to me and Zoe like she had the right to be there, and I didn't have the heart to tell her to push off.

Every time Kerry spoke, Zoe just looked stunned, as if she'd been punched in the face. She finally got me on my own in the girls' toilets at the end of break. 'What the hell happened?' Zoe demanded. 'How come we have that big klutz following around like she suddenly owns us?'

I confessed about the cross-country walk.

'You asked her?' Zoe smacked her hand on her forehead and swore. 'Are you mad? She won't leave us alone now. She'll think you're her best buddy.'

'She's OK, really,' I said. 'I think she's just lonely.'

Zoe shook her head and turned away from me. 'You sap.'

'Hey,' I said. 'Have you seen Kerry's brother?'

'Pasty Boy?' Zoe wrinkled her slender nose. 'What about him?'

I followed her out into the corridor. 'Nothing,' I said. 'We just saw him yesterday, that's all.'

Zoe turned to me with eyes like tiny knives. 'Tell me you don't fancy him?'

'Course not.'

'You've gone red.'

'Don't be stupid,' I said. 'It's just hot in here.'

Zoe was right, of course, about everything. After that day Kerry clung to us like that sticky weed that attaches itself to your clothes and won't be brushed away. And I did kind of like Kerry's brother.

Funny, though. We thought we'd never get rid of Kerry. Now, it's getting harder to see her real face in my head. Only the picture from the police posters is really clear.

24

3

And Jodie

I started spending all my Saturday mornings with Zoe, hanging around Dead Bouquet and the little cafe nearby, wishing we had more money. That's where we met Jodie. That name didn't suit her: it was too pretty and sunny. She was working at the shop one weekend when we went in and I sort of recognised her: she lived somewhere near us, because I'd seen her using The Cut. She was tall and skinny like a cardboard cut-out, her skin pale as if she'd been carved from a lump of grey-white candlewax. And the carver hadn't taken much trouble: her nose was so flat it almost didn't stick out of her face and her eyes were stone-coloured and lashless. She had a deep scar down one cheek that looked like someone had crumpled up her skin and forgotten to smooth it out again. Zoe called her Scarface, behind her back, of course, and to be honest, it suited her better than Jodie.

We'd got to the shop around ten o'clock in the morning when it had just opened up. No one else was in there. We did our usual routine of wandering round picking everything up, looking at the price in the useless hope that it had gone down since last week, then putting it down again. Sometimes we sneaked a sample of the tiny bottles of perfume oils, which you weren't supposed to do because they weren't testers like in the high street shops. And they were fearsomely expensive, with names like Dark Medicine, Death of Summer, and Absinthe Roses. We'd sniff them every week, make swooning gestures and sometimes get a dab on our wrists, if no one was looking.

But this morning, just after it opened, only we were in the shop and Jodie was watching us all the time. Eventually she said: 'Is there anything in particular you actually want?'

I looked at Zoe. Fact was, there was very little in the shop we could ever afford.

'We're just browsing,' Zoe said, wandering up to the counter and leaning on it. 'We come every weekend. We love this shop.'

Jodie was expressionless. She didn't even blink.

'You don't usually work here, do you?' Zoe went on. I went up to join her at the counter, because Zoe's chatter was making Jodie watch me even more carefully. I was sure she thought I wanted to pinch something.

Jodie shook her head. 'No, I don't. I'm just helping someone out for the day. Friend of a friend.'

'Would that be Geena?' Zoe was persistent, even though Jodie was talking in the kind of clipped tone that told me she didn't want to have a conversation. 'Geena owns the shop, doesn't she? She knows me quite well because I'm in here all the time.'

Zoe adored Geena, the goth-queen owner of Dead Bouquet, with her flawless make-up and her berry-coloured hair. Trying to impress Geena was the only time Zoe dropped her ice-queen pose.

'Yeah, Geena, that's right.' Jodie wasn't giving anything away.

'Shall I go and get you a coffee from the cafe? I sometimes do that for Geena,' Zoe offered.

'No, thanks.' Jodie picked up some flyers and patted them into a tidier pile.

I was sure we were getting on her nerves and I tried to make a face at Zoe, to get her to shut up. It didn't work. Zoe was making out that we were practically part-time staff at Dead Bouquet.

'OK if we try some of the clothes?' Zoe asked. Later in the morning there'd be a queue for the tiny little changing cubicle and Geena wasn't keen on us trying things on, because we never shelled out in the end.

Jodie shrugged. 'Long as you put them back properly.'

We spent about half an hour picking out some of the most gorgeous things on the rack. There was a black jacket with a kind of a bustle that made Zoe look like a Victorian schoolmistress and there was a full-length leather coat that trailed on the floor behind me. There was a black spiderweb cape and an amazing tartan mini dress that would even make my mum draw the line. It was just like being a kid again, with a huge dressing-up box.

'If I had hundreds of pounds I'd buy all of these,' said Zoe, stroking the spiderweb lace. 'Every single thing.'

Jodie almost smiled, but not quite.

The weird thing was that we saw Jodie again, just a few days later. We were walking home from school through The Cut, with Kerry tagging along as usual, and Jodie was standing there, leaning against a bare bit of fence, smoking a cigarette. She dipped her head as we went past, but we recognised her.

'Hi,' Zoe said. 'Scarface,' she hissed to me, from the side of her mouth.

Jodie mumbled something and sucked hard on the cigarette.

I stopped. I can tell when someone's been crying and they're trying to hide it. 'You all right?'

'I'm fine.' She sniffed loudly.

Zoe shook her head at me, to get me to keep walking, but I'm hopeless if someone's upset. I just can't walk past and leave them to it. I put my hand on her arm. She was much taller than me, but thin as a paper straw. She wasn't that much older than us, I reckoned – probably only around eighteen.

Jodie gave me a sort of a smile. 'Just a bit of a row with my boyfriend.'

She told us she lived in the high-rise flats on the edge of our estate, with this boyfriend. She'd come out for a walk because he was in a bad mood.

'I didn't think anyone was still in those flats,' I said. 'They look all boarded up.'

Jodie blew out smoke and sniffed again. 'They're trying to get everyone out. They're going to knock the flats down. But we're still there, until we find something else.'

'Are you going to work in Dead Bouquet again?' Zoe asked.

Jodie shook her head. 'Don't think so. I was just helping out because Geena was ill. Usually I work in Fryin' Chicken.' Now that she mentioned it, there was a smell of meat and cooking oil hanging around her.

'I love that stuff,' Kerry said. Zoe made a face behind her back. 'But my mum hates it. She says it's too expensive and full of fat.'

Jodie smiled at Kerry. 'She might be right.'

'Are you OK, really?' I asked Jodie.

Jodie threw her cigarette butt onto the ground and stamped on it lightly. 'Yeah. Thanks. I just needed some air.'

She started walking away. Then she stopped and turned. 'Hey,' she said. 'Come round tomorrow after school. I always get a load of chicken to take home. I get sick of the stuff. You can help me eat it.'

Zoe scribbled down the number of the flat on the back of her hand.

The next day, we were a bit tense and giggly, full of a weird excitement. Zoe and I had stuffed a change of clothes into our school bags, but Kerry hadn't thought about that, so she was still in her school uniform as we went towards Jodie's house. It was just as well: Kerry always looked even more of an embarrassment than usual out of school. The grey and black uniform was boring, but at least it made everyone look as rubbish as each other, even the really cool girl gangs, because they had to wear regulation shoes, tone down their hair colours and they weren't supposed to wear make-up. But what you wore out of school said a bit more about you. Zoe wore things that were a bit eccentric, that she made herself, and looked good in a 'so-sue-me' sort of a way. My mum was a bit soft – especially since the divorce – and when she got paid she could be persuaded to buy me clothes that I wanted and wouldn't get me laughed at. But Kerry. Her mum bought her supermarket jeans that made her look like an overgrown kid or else someone aged over fifty, so high-waisted they nearly reached her armpits. She wore her tops buttoned up to the neck – that was something to do with what they were told at her church.

I badly wanted to see Jodie's home and so did Zoe. Kerry just wanted to do what we were doing. Also, Zoe had done this amazing manga drawing that looked just like Jodie, only with big eyes and a mane of hair. In fact, it made her look like some kind of beautiful cartoon superhero, which she didn't in real life.

The high rises were even worse than we'd expected, because so many people had moved out and most of the doors and windows were covered in metal panels and graffiti. The stench on the staircase was really bad: stale fag smoke and damp and pee. We had to take the lift because Jodie's flat was on the ninth floor. I don't like heights, so I tried not to think about how far up we were going and the way the lift made a grinding noise, like it might break down at any minute. Zoe told us we'd see the place littered with needles, because the high rises had a bad reputation for drugs. We didn't actually see any needles – that was one of Zoe's exaggerations – but it did stink.

Jodie opened the door and the thick smell of Fryin' Chicken wafted out. 'Brilliant,' said Kerry. Inside, as well as the smell of the food, there was a kind of a mustiness in the air that reminded me of my nan's outhouse.

Zoe handed Jodie the drawing. 'I can't pay you for the food,' she told her. 'I'm an impoverished artist.'

Jodie's lips twitched at the sides. 'Right. Whatever that means.'

'So I did this sketch of you. You never know, it might be worth money when I'm famous.'

Jodie unrolled the paper. She shook her head and said it was amazing. She even went a bit teary-eyed and I could tell Zoe loved having that effect on her. 'My Dave's got a tattoo on his back that looks a bit like that,' Jodie told us.

The room didn't have much furniture, but there was a little low table that was covered with the bright yellow boxes that the chicken came in, a pile of paper napkins and three big cartons of drinks. We ate the food in our hands, sitting on the floor. It made our fingers slippery with grease. Kerry sucked her fingers so hard that I told her she'd soon have no fingerprints left. Zoe glared as if she'd like to smack Kerry's hands.

From Jodie's window, you could see all across the whole of Shieldsgate: our own streets and then right across the motorway, the steeple of the cathedral and some of the taller buildings, like the council offices and the university. I felt dizzy standing next to the window and it even made my nerves tingle when Kerry pressed her nose to the glass. Zoe, though, could hardly tear herself away from it. She said one day she was going to live in a penthouse flat with a view like this one. She said it would have her artist's studio in it and she would paint the scene from the window.

Jodie snorted at the word 'penthouse'. When the door opened and her boyfriend Dave came in, she said: 'Welcome to the penthouse,' and sniggered.

He said: 'What are you on about?'

Then he looked at us. 'Hello, ladies.' His voice went into a drawl.

Kerry giggled.

'Some men wouldn't be happy about coming home and finding the room full of schoolgirls,' Dave said, more to Jodie than to us, and I thought there was a bit of a knife-edge in his voice. Then he laughed. 'But I'm not complaining.'

Zoe and I caught each other's glance. Dave coming in made the whole room feel a bit different. Also, I'd noticed Zoe usually got weird around boys. She always went really quiet, like she was closing the doors on herself. She just went over to the window again and gazed out as if she was looking at the New York skyline or something, not our cruddy east end.

Dave wasn't as tall as Jodie, but he was thin and muscly. When we pestered him, he took off his shirt and showed us the tattoo across his back, but it wasn't much like Zoe's drawing after all. Then he sat without a top on for the rest of the time, which made me feel like I shouldn't even be looking at him.

I wished I hadn't gone to the bathroom because I saw things like boxes of tampons and packets of condoms. I didn't want to think about all that stuff between Jodie and Dave. It made me twist inside, as if I had something to be ashamed of.

When I came back into the living room, Kerry was babbling about how she should have changed out of her school uniform. 'I'm not complaining,' Dave said, again. Zoe looked at me and twisted her lip.

It was getting dusky outside. Dave asked us if we wanted some beer. That was when Zoe said we had to get Kerry back home. Kerry said she was fine, and Dave pulled four cans out of a plastic bag, but Zoe glared at her until she said, 'Oh, well, maybe we'd better go.'

We pressed and pressed the button for the lift, but it didn't come, so we clattered our way down nine flights of chilly concrete steps. 'I came here once before, a couple of years ago,' Zoe said. 'Someone at school asked me round. It was bad then, but it's worse now.'

'Probably because they want to pull the flats down anyway,' I said.

'I think they should knock them down,' Kerry said, shivering. 'They feel horrible.'

Zoe sighed. 'You're a philistine,' she said.

'A what?'

'What they should do,' Zoe said, 'is fix them all up properly and rent them out as artists' studios. I'd live in one if I could. That view is awesome. I'm going to ask Jodie if I can come back and paint it.'

I just didn't have Zoe's imagination, I reckoned, because I couldn't see anything but misery in the place. The damp and cold of the staircases gave us all goosebumps. We couldn't wait to get out into the fresh air.

4

Birthday

In early June, it was coming up for Zoe's birthday. It was the first time I realised she was older than me. Kerry confided Zoe had been kept back a year, because she'd had so much time off. Zoe spotted a flyer for a gig with three different local goth bands. She was desperate to go.

'That's all I want to do for my birthday,' she said, waving the leaflet at me as we sat on our coats on the damp low wall at school during morning break. 'I wouldn't want presents or anything if I could just go to that gig.'

I squeezed her lightly on the shoulder. I'd guessed there was no way Zoe's mum would allow it. From the way Zoe described things, her mum's mission in life was to make Zoe miserable. Mine probably would've agreed, as long as my dad could pick me up at the end of it. But Zoe's mum had said a flat no. The tickets were £20 each. I could have eked it out of my dad, if I'd worked on him for a bit, but Zoe never had any cash at all.

Kerry frowned at the flyer. 'I've never heard of any of these bands,' she said. 'How do you know they're not rubbish, anyway?'

Zoe made a low growling noise in her throat.

'Why don't we do something else?' Kerry said, trying to get Zoe to cheer up and going exactly the wrong way about it.

'Such as?' Zoe turned to Kerry and her eyes were icy diamonds. 'What would you like to do? Play Scrabble with big brother? Go to church and sing some hymns?'

Kerry went pink. She did go to church, every weekend and even sometimes during the week. Zoe teased her about it, when she was bored enough to pay Kerry any attention.

'I thought maybe we could all go out and have a pizza or something,' Kerry said, in a sort of a mumble, because I think she already knew Zoe was going to shoot her down.

'Why the hell would I want to do that? Why would I want to spend my birthday listening to you? It's bad enough every other day.'

'Zoe,' I said, shifting my legs. The cold from the brick wall was starting to make me feel numb. 'Don't.'

Kerry looked like she'd been slapped. 'I just wanted to –'

'Just shut up!' Zoe shouted. Really shouted. Both Kerry and I jumped.

Kerry got up and said something about going to the toilet.

'I know you're going to cry, stupid baby,' Zoe called after her. Kerry didn't turn around.

I looked at Zoe. She blinked and screwed up her eyes. 'What's up?' I asked, giving her a gentle nudge with my elbow.

Zoe shook her head and said nothing. She was staring down at the ground, so hard that I looked to see what was there.

'Is it your mum?'

Zoe shrugged. 'No more than usual.' Her hair was drooping down at either side of her face, hiding her expression.

'I wish I could get you to that gig,' I said. 'I'd love to go too.'

Zoe sniffed and looked up. 'Yeah?'

I nodded.

'I was thinking,' Zoe said. 'If I said I was staying with you – and you said you were, I don't know, staying with someone else, maybe we could go to the gig.'

I thought about this. 'How, though?'

'Suppose I got the money for the tickets.'

'But how would you -?'

'Never mind that for now. Just suppose I did. Would you be up for it?'

I felt something like pins and needles creeping through my body. 'If we went to the gig, and you were meant to be staying with me, where would we go for the rest of the night?'

Zoe looked at me. 'We could ask Jodie. I bet she'd let us crash on her floor.'

'What about that Dave, though? He gives me the creeps.'

'Me too. But it'd just be for one night. We could stick together. We'd be fine.'

'I could ask my dad if he'd pick us up and take us back to mine?'

Zoe wrinkled her nose. 'Too embarrassing. We'd look like little kids.'

'How would you get the ticket money then?'

Zoe looked away from me. 'I've got a birthday coming up, remember? I'm bound to get some cash from somewhere. That's just a detail, anyway. Are you in?'

I didn't dare hesitate. 'I'm in.'

Zoe grabbed my hand and squeezed it. 'We haven't got to mention this to Pizza Face,' she said.

'Kerry? No. Sure. But, Zoe –'

The lesson bell made us both groan. Zoe got up from the wall and pulled me up after her. 'Finally,' she said. 'Something's going to happen. I have a reason for living after all.'

I laughed as we ran back to the class, brushing damp and grit from my coat.

I'd already bought Zoe a birthday present. It was a little pewter box lined with red velvet. Inside, wrapped in black tissue paper, was a phial of a scent called Poisoned Wine, which was her favourite of the ones we always sampled in the shop every weekend. It came with a little scroll of paper listing its ingredients: things like amber, patchouli and something called dragon's blood. She was going to love it.

Kerry told me she'd bought Zoe a postcard of the Shieldsgate skyline at night and that she'd put it in a frame. 'It looks really like the view from Jodie's window,' she said. 'Do you think Zoe will be pleased?'

''Course she will,' I said. I was a bit jealous of this idea myself, though you couldn't really guess how Zoe would react to anything Kerry gave her.

'What is she going to do on her birthday?' Kerry was good at forgetting, or seeming to forget, most of the times when Zoe was cruel to her. A couple of hours later she was always bouncing back at us.

I shrugged.

'Why doesn't she want to go for a pizza?' Kerry asked. 'It'd be good.'

She just doesn't want to go with you, I thought. 'Zoe never has any money,' I said.

'I would treat her for her birthday,' Kerry said.

I made a face. 'I don't know, Kerry. I think she'd be embarrassed about that.'

'My brother's started working weekends in this brilliant new Italian place in town,' Kerry said. 'It pays better than the bakery because he gets tips.'

I sat up at the mention of Luke. 'Really? Where?'

'Near the library. The menu looks gorgeous. He said I should bring you along.'

'He did?' I felt a little electric charge go through me. 'Honest?'

Kerry nodded. 'I'm sure he meant Zoe as well,' she said.

I thought for a second. 'But he just mentioned me?'

'Yeah, he said he really likes you.'

'Truly?'

Kerry blinked at me, like it was no big deal. 'Of course. He says it's great that I've got some mates after all this time.' She lowered her eyes. 'It was tough, you know, never having anyone to hang around with. When it was really bad, Luke sometimes came to meet me after school. To make sure no one *got* me. You know.'

I did know. Maxine and her mates would go for anyone who looked at them the wrong way, if they were in the mood. I felt a guilty twinge inside. Fact was, whenever we could, Zoe and I tried to lose Kerry. And we never asked her out with us at weekends. I knew Zoe wouldn't be seen with someone like Kerry when she was trying to fit in with the Dead Bouquet crowd.

'Look,' I said. 'I'll try to persuade Zoe to go. Can't promise, though.'

So later I started working on Zoe, which wasn't easy. I told her that Kerry had already booked us a table. I suggested we could go there early and then go on to the gig.

Zoe pulled a face. 'Yes, but what if Kerry follows us? We can't tell anyone else what we're doing. You know we'll be in it up to our necks if my mother finds out.'

I gave Zoe puppy-dog eyes.

She covered her face and shook her head. 'Stop it! It's my birthday we're talking about. Don't make me spend it with Pollyanna!'

In the end, we agreed that we'd do it, on the condition that I didn't say a word to Kerry about where we were going afterwards.

5

The gig

On the night of Zoe's birthday, a Saturday, we must've spent two hours getting ready. Zoe came to my house and we'd concocted a story for our mums which involved having a sleepover at someone from school's house. We'd even agreed on a name – Emma Wood – but the girl we were supposed to be staying with didn't exist and the mobile number I left with my mum was completely made up. I was banking on the fact that she wasn't going to check. I felt a bit sick about it, to be honest. But Zoe had bought the tickets and whenever Kerry was out of earshot, she'd talked about nothing else for days.

In my bedroom, we spoke in low voices. 'Did Jodie say we could stay at her house then?'

Zoe was sitting at my mirror painting on her gloss-black eyeliner into perfect symmetrical flicks at the corner of each eye. 'Sort of.'

I pulled my T-shirt over my head and smoothed out the creases. 'Sort of? What do you mean by "sort of"?'

Zoe looked in the mirror at my reflection, staring at her. 'Well, she told us we could come round any time, didn't she? Ages ago.'

'You mean she doesn't actually know we're coming tonight, late?'

Zoe shrugged. 'She'll be all right. It's not going to be like turning up at your gran's house.'

My insides squirmed again. 'Zoe...'

She held up a pale hand, her nails painted a heavy shade of purple. 'Don't. It's my birthday. Don't spoil it.' She started conducting with her mascara brush, along with the track playing in the background.

I swallowed my words back down.

Zoe turned to me. Her hair shone and her eyes glinted behind their perfectly-flicked eyeliner. She looked more beautiful than I'd ever seen her. 'Hey,' she said. 'That present was the best ever.' She dabbed some of the scented oil on to her wrists and held the phial out to me. 'Want some?'

I shook my head. I'd already borrowed a splash of my mum's designer stuff. She hardly ever used it, so I reckoned it was only going to go off if I didn't help out.

By the time we got to the restaurant we were about half an hour late. Kerry was standing outside, her face all red and blotchy. She was wearing this floaty white top that looked completely wrong on her because she was so big and bulky. And she looked freezing. 'You're here,' she said.

Zoe glanced over her shoulder. 'Looks like it.'

'I thought you weren't coming. I thought you'd just gone off somewhere else without me.'

'We wouldn't do that,' I lied. 'Sorry. The bus was late.'

We went inside. I really liked the decor because it was a bit goth-y and the smell of garlic made my stomach feel suddenly empty. The tables and chairs were a dark wood, the walls were deep red and there were elaborate candlesticks with drooping, worn candles in them.

Zoe gave a sigh. 'Mock-goth,' she said.

'This looks great,' I said, hoping to cheer Kerry up. She sat down and handed Zoe a flat parcel wrapped in shiny paper. Zoe gave her a fake smile and pulled at the paper. She raised her eyebrows when she saw what it was. 'Hey,' she said. 'That's actually quite nice.'

'I thought you could paint the view from the photo,' Kerry said.

Zoe shook her head. 'No, I couldn't, Kerry. It would be copying someone else's art. Photos are art too, you know. It's not the done thing.'

I turned away from Kerry's disappointed face because I could see Luke coming towards us. I felt that odd little jolt inside. I lifted the menu to hide my face and stared as if I was about to be tested on the choices. It was more expensive than I'd expected.

'Umm, Kerry,' I said. 'It's not exactly cheap and cheerful, is it?'

Kerry grinned at us. 'I'm treating us all, remember? I'm getting Luke's staff discount too, so it's not as bad as it looks.'

I winced. Zoe gave a small smile. 'If you insist. I'd like this black pasta stuff, please.'

It was the most expensive thing on the menu. I noticed Kerry flinch, just a little, but she didn't say anything. I sought out the plainest, cheapest pasta on the list.

Luke was hovering, notebook in hand.

'And a bottle of your finest red wine,' Zoe said to him and he laughed.

'No can do, ladies. Try again.' He looked at me. 'Hi again. Anna, right?'

I felt like my tongue was glued down. 'Yeah, hi. Plain tomato pasta, please. Actually – I'm not all that hungry. Do you do half-portions?'

Zoe pursed her lips. 'Anna, Kerry's treating us. Don't be so rude. A few minutes ago you told me you were starving.'

Kerry smiled at me. 'It's fine, you have whatever you want.'

Luke looked at his sister. 'You're paying for all of this?'

Kerry shifted in her seat. 'It's Zoe's birthday.'

'I can pay for myself,' I chipped in.

'No,' said Kerry and she gave her brother a glare. 'I promised.'

Zoe pressed her lips together as if she wanted to laugh.

Luke took our orders and went off to the kitchen to bring us some iced water.

I wasn't lying. The combination of the menu prices and seeing Luke again had kind of killed my appetite. And I could feel Zoe watching me.

The food was really good, though, and Luke brought us a free plate of warm bread and green olives to go with it. When he smiled at me, very directly, I went a bit hot in the face. As soon as he'd gone, though, Zoe dropped her fork into her bowl of pasta, with a loud clatter. Black-ish sauce like ink spots splattered onto the table cloth. Kerry jumped and checked her white top.

'Say it ain't so, Anna. Tell me there's nothing going on between you and the bread boy.'

'That's my brother,' said Kerry. 'He's called Luke.'

Zoe closed her eyes. 'I know that. So what?'

Kerry shrugged and looked down at her plate. I knew how she felt. Sometimes Zoe could be a bit scary. She was so much worse to Kerry than to anyone else, though.

''Course there's nothing going on,' I said. 'I met him once before, that's all. Kerry, this food is amazing. I love this place.'

'Well, I don't,' Zoe said, pushing her bowl away. 'It's pretentious. It's just Presto Pasta with tacky faux-goth decor. And it's over-priced.'

'That shouldn't matter, seeing as how you're not paying,' said a voice beside us and we looked round to see Luke next to the table. He'd even brought a little cake, lit with a sparkler. 'Kerry organised this for you,' he said.

Zoe looked at it as if it was a dog turd with a candle in it, pushed back her chair and stood up. 'And it's staffed by morons.' She turned to me. 'I think we have a gig to go on to.'

I cringed. 'Give me a minute,' I said.

'See you outside then.' Zoe strode to the door.

I didn't know where to look or what to say. 'Kerry, I'm sorry, I don't know what's the matter with her. I thought it was all lovely, honest, I did.'

Luke started picking up the plates and piling them up into one hand. Kerry was still sitting staring into her half-eaten food. 'I thought she'd really like it,' she said, almost in a whisper.

I reached across the table and squeezed her hand. 'I know. It was nice of you. She's just... it's not you. It's her.'

She looked up. 'Where are you going to now?'

I ran my hands through my hair. It was so hot in this place. 'Just a gig. A couple of college goth bands, that's all. We – we didn't think you'd like that sort of thing.'

'You never asked, though.'

I could tell from the thickness of her voice that Kerry was close to crying, and I desperately wanted to stop her. 'We should've done. We will next time.'

Kerry must've known I was lying about that. She glanced at her watch. 'It's nearly ten o'clock. What time does it start?'

I shrugged. 'It goes on till late.'

'Did Zoe's mother say she could go, then?' Kerry asked, sniffing.

'No, of course not. We're supposed to be somewhere else for the night. Don't tell anyone, for god's sake.' I dug into my bag. 'Here.' I pulled out some money. 'I don't want you to have to pay for this.'

Kerry shook her head. I dropped the notes on the table and stood up. As I was scurrying out, I passed Luke on his way to another table. I stopped and looked up at him. 'I'm really sorry,' I said. 'We never meant to upset Kerry. I feel awful.'

'It wasn't you, it was your spooky mate,' Luke said. 'But you could've asked Kerry along to the gig with you. She's quite –' He glanced over to make sure she wasn't watching. 'She gets lonely, that's all. I want her to have a friend. Friends.'

'I know,' I said. My insides felt heavy, as if something was pulling me down.

Outside, it was darker than it should have been, because it had barely got light all day. There was a smell of rain in the air and a deep grey sky without stars. Zoe was shivering. 'I thought you were never coming. I thought you must've stayed for dessert. Cake and jelly with Kerry and her sad sibling.'

'Sorry.'

We started walking, fast, towards the university bar where the gig was being held. I took a big, inward breath. 'Zoe, did you have to be like that with Kerry? She was trying so hard to do something for you. To please you.'

'Well, I wish she wouldn't,' Zoe said. 'I don't want her hanging around with us, you know that. And the more we put up with her, the more she'll keep plaguing us. I'm being cruel to be kind, that's all. I keep hoping that one day she'll get the message.'

We kept marching, because it was so chilly, and I tried to push the memory of Kerry's face out of my mind. And Luke's face, too.

There was a small crowd at the entrance to the university bar, all looking like the kind of people who hung around Dead Bouquet, their usual heavy, sweet smell fighting the dampness in the air. A student wearing a T-shirt, with Gothic Winter, the name of one of the bands, on the front, came up and offered us tickets for a fiver each.

'You're joking,' said Zoe. 'I paid twenty quid last week.'

The girl shrugged. 'I know, but there aren't many people here. We're just trying to get more bodies in through the door.'

We pushed our way in and Zoe spotted someone she knew from the shop. She had a word with them and came back to me with a grin. 'They're going to get us some drinks,' she said. 'We'd never get served otherwise.'

'What're they getting?' All I wanted was a long drink of cold water.

'Wait and see.'

Zoe's friend came back after quite a while with two tall glasses full of black liquid. 'Two Gravedigger cocktails,' she said, laughing, and gave Zoe some change.

I sniffed at mine and wrinkled my nose. 'What the heck's in here?'

'Best not to ask,' Zoe said. She took a sip, swallowed and screwed up her eyes. 'It's nice. Just don't drink it too fast.'

I took a tiny taste and winced as the sourness burned the back of my throat. 'That's unlikely.'

There was a loud, grinding squeal as the next band tested their mikes and, as the music started, people started moving forward towards the stage. Zoe grabbed my wrist and pulled me towards the front, where the sound was ear-splitting, but she didn't seem to care. Then Zoe started to dance.

I'd never seen her dance before – just sometimes nodding her head along to a track. It was like watching a different person. Zoe, who was always so cool and so careful, was like a mad, beautiful sprite, her long hair around her face, the black lace of her dress fluttering around her like moth wings. I was bobbing around next to her, feeling about as graceful as a lump of wood. In the middle of the song, the singer reached his hand down from the stage and beckoned her to come up. She leapt up without a second's pause and danced on the stage. People were whistling and clapping. I stopped even trying to dance and just sort of shuffled my feet, my gaze never leaving Zoe.

At the end of the set, the lead singer slipped his arm around Zoe's waist and leaned over to kiss her, so that she fell backwards in an old-film-style swoon, and he held her up. Then she took her own bow. I was clapping and shrieking louder than anyone. I had half an urge to turn around and yell out to everyone that she was my friend. I was so proud to know her. When she stepped down from the stage she ran straight towards me and we hugged.

'That was amazing. You were fantastic,' I told her. We went to get some water and I used the edge of my sleeve to wipe the little black smears where her eyeliner and mascara had run. Zoe's eyes widened and I turned to see the singer from the band heading towards us. He was wearing a black dinner suit, a top hat and pale face make-up, streaked with sweat.

'Hey,' he said. 'That was pretty good. Can I get you a drink?'

Zoe nodded. 'Two Gravediggers,' she said, ignoring the way I was wrinkling my nose. When he turned towards the bar, she opened her mouth in a silent, excited scream. I made a face back at her. I liked all the gothy clothes and music and everything, but I found the guys a bit creepy. I didn't think I could seriously fancy anyone who went to all that trouble to dress like a Victorian undertaker. But Zoe obviously did.

The singer came back with two more tall glasses of the dreaded black stuff. He asked our names and what we were studying. He thought we were university students. Zoe told him, without batting her heavily crayoned eyelids, that she was doing an art degree.

'I thought you might be a professional dancer,' the guy said. I stuck my tongue out at Zoe, but she was too busy gazing at him to notice. He said his name was Tom and for some reason this made me want to laugh, because it was such a normal name for a weird-looking guy. 'Do you fancy coming along to some more of our gigs and dancing on the stage? It just went down really well. We'll give you a few quid – can't be more, because we don't get that much ourselves. But it goes with the whole act.'

Zoe looked like she'd won the Lottery. I watched as she scribbled Tom's number on her hand. It was definitely not the time to remind her that her mother would never let her out to be the dancer in a student band. Or that it was only a matter of time before Band-Boy realised she was only just sixteen.

There were other people standing around with us, including the band's two guitarists and some girls who were closer to them in age. I listened in to some of their chat, but it was pretty hard to hear anything properly, because there were so many people there by now and another band had started their set. I turned to see if Zoe wanted to move back towards the stage again. She was in a clinch with Tom. It took me a second to realise what was happening, but she was enveloped by his long black body and spidery arms. It looked almost like he was eating her alive.

'*Eeeeuw,*' I said out loud, not that anyone heard me or took any notice. I didn't quite know where to put myself, so without really needing to, I made for the toilets. It took ages to squeeze myself through the crowd and then there was a queue. It was when I'd finally got myself into a cubicle that I heard my mobile ringtone. I pulled it out of my bag and the display read: Mum. It also said there'd been six missed calls – all from Mum. My heart started thumping. I started to dial her back, my fingers shaky, when I realised I'd better talk to Zoe first. If someone had checked up on us, then we'd better get our stories straight.

I clicked the mobile off and pushed my painfully slow way back towards the bar, craning my neck to see if I could spot Zoe and grab her attention as fast as possible. I couldn't see her anywhere – or the singer. After a few minutes of searching, I started to panic. I tried skirting round the dark corners of the hall to see if she and Tom were tucked away somewhere together, but I couldn't find them anywhere. The noise of the band, the flashing lights and smells of beer and sweat and hairspray were making me feel shaky and sick. Eventually I recognised the Gothic Winter guitarist, next to a girl with an Elvira-style hairdo. I tapped his arm and tried to ask where his lead singer was, although I had to yell at him and wave my hands about and he didn't seem very bothered or interested. He smiled and blinked blearily, as if I'd just woken him up.

Elvira shook her towering hairdo at me. 'He's probably taken her back to the van. Your friend should know she's just one of a long list of notches on his bed post, darling.'

'Where's the van?' I shouted.

Elvira took my arm and steered me towards a fire exit. I followed someone with a guitar case out of the double doors and into a small car park. Outside, the cool air felt like water. I took a huge breath and wiped my sweaty, grimy face. I could only see a couple of vans. The guy with the case went towards one of them and threw open the back, which was full of boxes and stuff. I ran over to the other van, but it was dark and empty. I rapped on the window, but I could see there was no one inside. The rest of the cark park was deserted – no other vehicles, apart from a battered motorbike. My stomach felt as if a brick was sinking deep down into it. I fished out my phone and texted her. *Wr r u???* I waited a few moments, muttering at the phone as if that would make it ping, but there was no reply.

I turned back to the stuffy concert bar, the music pounding in my head and the smells of booze feeling overpowering. The guy behind the bar said he hadn't seen her, nor had the girl on the entrance door and she wasn't in the toilets. Elvira scribbled Tom's number down for me on a flyer and I tried calling that, but I just got some spaced-out voicemail message. My own phone said there'd now been eight missed calls and they were all from Mum. I was going to have to call her back.

Outside, I could hardly tap in the numbers because my fingers were trembling so much. She was going to go absolutely wild with me. And I couldn't think of a way to speak to Mum without getting Zoe into a shed-load of trouble too. I tried texting her again. *Crisis, nd 2 spk 2 u asap.*

The phone at home rang and rang. There was no answer. I tried again, but the ringtone just kept going. I could see the battery on my mobile getting low.

I started trudging away from the concert hall, without any real idea what I was going to do. Rain spat down on me. I was going in the direction of the bus stop, but I

51

wasn't even sure there were any buses running, because it was well after midnight. There were plenty of people around, but all in big groups, staggering between bars and clubs, their shouts coming in waves of sound. I was cold through to the bone and shuddering. I felt like the slightest thing would make me throw up.

As I stood at the bus stop, shivering, blinking back tears, ignoring the drunken lads lumbering past, I heard a car horn beeping and looked up. It was Dad's car and I could see that Mum was in the passenger seat. They pulled the car up into the bus bay and Mum gestured for me to get in.

As soon as I threw myself onto the back seat, with its fuggy warmth and familiar Dad-smell, I burst into tears. I don't really know what made that happen. Dad started the car again and we drove off towards our house. Dad said nothing at first. It was Mum who fired off all the questions.

'What on earth did you think you were doing? Why didn't you tell me where you were really going? And where's Zoe? Her mother is going out of her mind with worry too, just like us.'

I sniffed and swallowed, trying to summon up the sense and the energy to answer. 'I'm sorry, Mum. Sorry, Dad.'

Dad just gave me a look in the rear-view mirror and shook his head.

I tried to explain that we just went to a concert and we'd planned to stay with a friend. But she hadn't turned up, I said. I was making it up as I went along, of course.

'Why did you call me anyway?' I asked Mum. 'Has something happened?'

Mum shuffled round in her seat to glare at me. 'What happened is that I had a frantic phone call from Zoe's mother asking if she was at our house. It seems some girl turned up at the door and told her mother she'd gone off to a concert and Zoe's mother wasn't too happy about it. Then I couldn't raise you on the mobile. What was going on in your head, Anna? And where is Zoe anyway? Please tell me she's gone home already.'

I found I was crying again and I shook my head. 'I sort of lost her at the concert, Mum. I don't know where she went.'

Mum and Dad looked at each other. The car indicator gave its gentle ticking sound and Dad pulled the car into a side street where he could turn around. 'I guess we're going back to look for Zoe, then.'

Just then my mobile pinged. I squinted at it in the dark. It was a number I didn't recognise sending me a text. *Z here. Mob flat. This is Toms. Wr r u now?*

I replied. *Wr r u???*

Outside bar. Cm & get me?

I decided not to tell her I was bringing my parents with me, in case she panicked. I got them to go to the back of the building where the little car park was and I jumped out and ran to the front. Zoe was on her own, waiting for me and when she saw me she gave me a squashy hug. 'Sorry,' she said. She smelled of Tom's cigarette smoke.

'Where's Dracula?' I asked.

She shrugged. 'Tom had to get off. I've got his number though. Hey, what's up?'

I shook my head. 'Bad news.' I told her what had happened. For some reason, though, I decided not to mention that someone – Kerry, almost certainly – had deliberately dropped her in trouble. Instead I just told her

53

that her mum was looking for her and that my parents were parked around the corner.

Zoe groaned. 'I don't suppose we can make a run for it?'

I grasped her arm and steered her towards the car park. 'Don't be stupid.'

When we got into the car, I tried my best to persuade my mum to let Zoe stay the night, but she wouldn't hear of it. Dad dropped Zoe off outside her house and watched as she put her key in the door, in spite of Zoe's claims that she wouldn't get away from her mum alive.

Later, over a cup of tea, I told Mum I was sorry, about a hundred times. She lectured me for a few minutes, but once Dad went, she got over it pretty fast. I think she was just relieved that she'd found me.

'What was Zoe's mum like?' I asked.

My mum paused. 'Angry.'

'Yeah, I know. But what did you make of her?'

Mum stuck out her lower lip and I could see her choosing her words. 'If you first speak to someone when they're beside themselves with worry, it's too hard to tell what they're like. I could understand why she was so furious. I don't care if they don't get on. Zoe shouldn't have gone behind her mother's back like that. And I don't want you being part of it again, understand? For god's sake, anything could've happened to you.'

I hung my head. 'I know.'

I sipped my tea, which was going cold. 'Do you know who it was who dropped – I mean, who told Zoe's mum where we were?'

'I don't,' Mum said. 'But I'm sure she didn't mean to get Zoe into trouble. Maybe she was just worried about you both. Like I was.'

I stood up to go to bed. 'Mum,' I said. 'Dad didn't say much. Was he really mad with me?'

'A bit. But his girlfriend is even madder. They were having a romantic supper and we ruined it, from what I can gather.' Mum's mouth twitched. 'Shame.'

'Mum!' I shook my head at her and made for the stairs.

I can't remember when I was last so tired, but when I got into bed I couldn't relax enough to get to sleep. The whole evening kept racing round in my head: the awful scene in the restaurant with Kerry. The way Luke looked at me. Zoe, dancing. That vampiric singer trying to eat her up. Kerry's spiteful revenge. And Zoe's face as she got out of our car, squeezing my hand and then drawing her finger across her throat. She was expecting more than a telling off.

6

Trouble

After an almost sleepless night, I got up the next morning with my head feeling like it was full of mud. The first thing I did was text Zoe – *U k? Call me* – but I didn't get an answer. I made some tea and took a mug up to Mum. She was just coming out of her room, looking groggy. 'I didn't sleep. Did you?'

I shook my head.

She took the mug and blew on it. 'This doesn't make everything OK, Anna. I ought to ground you or something.'

'I know.'

Mum sighed. 'Lucky for you I don't have the energy. You're all I've got now. I'm not up for a big row.'

That made me feel worse than if she'd grounded me for the rest of the year, of course.

When I was dressed, I marched round to Kerry's house. As I knocked on her door, I realised I didn't really know what I was going to say to her, but I had to say something.

It was Kerry's mum who answered and she looked at me like I smelled bad, but she gave Kerry a shout. Kerry galloped to the door like a big clumsy Labrador and said 'Hi' as if last night had never happened. My mouth opened and I just stared at her for a second or two. Then I said: 'What the hell were you thinking?'

It didn't seem to matter that she was a good head and shoulders taller than me, about a stone heavier and as smart as a professor when it came to things like formulae and equations. Whenever I was hard on her, it felt like I was being mean to some little toddler.

'What are you talking about?' She went so pink in the face that even if I hadn't guessed it was Kerry who dropped Zoe in trouble, that would've given it away.

'You grassed on Zoe. You went to her house and told Zoe's mum where she was. She's in a whole load of trouble, thanks to you.'

Kerry looked down at her shoes. 'You don't know it was me.'

I gave a short laugh. 'Except it was, wasn't it? No one else knew, for one thing. It had to be you. Have you any idea what you've done?'

To be honest, even I didn't know exactly how things were with Zoe, but I could bet that her mum wouldn't be anything like as forgiving as mine.

Kerry's eyes went all watery and she shook her head. 'I was worried, that's all. I thought something might happen to you and no one else would know where you were.'

'We were fine. The problems only started when you went around stirring things up. Everyone went mad with us. My mum panicked and my dad had to go driving round looking for me in the middle of the night. I know Zoe was a complete cow. But there was no need for that.' I felt like shaking her.

Kerry let out a loud, snotty sob. 'I was just scared. What if –'

I clenched my fists and swallowed down my urge to shout. 'You want to hang round with us, don't you? You're going the wrong way about it.'

57

I swung around to leave, then turned back again. 'Zoe is going to kill you. You know that, don't you?'

Kerry slumped down on her front step and put her face in her hands. My phone buzzed and I read Zoe's text. It said: *Still alive. Just. C u Monday.*

I waved my mobile at Kerry. 'That's Zoe. She's having a really bad time. Hope you're happy.'

'Some people ask for trouble,' said a voice. Luke had just appeared at the door, behind Kerry. He looked as if he'd just showered, because his hair was damp and there was a soapy scent around him. He leaned down to give Kerry a gentle punch across the top of the head. Kerry looked up at him, scrunching back her tears with her eyelids. I silently groaned. How come he saw me when I was acting my worst?

'Look,' I said. 'Zoe was an idiot last night, especially in the restaurant. I was ashamed too, if you must know. But there was no need to do what you did.'

Kerry heaved herself up and wiped her face with the back of her hand. 'You've made your point,' she said and went indoors.

Luke stared down at the ground.

'I'm sorry,' I said to him. 'About last night, I mean. But –'

He gave a long outward sigh. 'She doesn't mean it,' he said. 'She just doesn't think things through. It comes from not having any real friends. You're the first ones who've let her anywhere near. She's a bit of a big kid, really. You and that Zoe are light years ahead of her. Just – you know – be a bit patient with her, all right?'

Guilt washed through me, a hot, sickly wave. 'I know,' I said. 'But maybe she ought to find someone else to –'

'Yeah, like who?' said Luke.

I thought for a minute. 'She goes to church, doesn't she? Isn't there anyone there?'

Luke made a face. 'I think she needs to get away from that.'

'Don't you go, then?'

Luke shook his head. 'It's my stepmum who got involved with that outfit. I've never had anything to do with it. It's not your usual church, you know. They have some funny ideas.'

I nodded, but I didn't have much of a clue what he meant, except I had heard Kerry say she'd been told not to read books about the supernatural because her church said it was wrong. She hadn't even read *Harry Potter*. I thought it sounded a bit weird. 'Hey, I loved the food last night,' I said. 'I think Zoe would, usually. She was all uptight about the concert and her birthday and stuff, that's all.'

Luke gave me a smile. I loved his smile. It made you have to give one back. 'Thanks. You're a good person, Anna. So you'll plead Kerry's case for her?'

I hadn't exactly said that, but – 'Yeah, I'll try. No promises though. Zoe doesn't get on with her mum at the best of times and this really won't have helped.'

'Thanks, you're a star.' Luke turned to go back inside. 'Next time you're in town, drop in again. I work Thursdays, Fridays and Saturdays.'

'It's a bit out of my price range, to be honest,' I said. Then I wished I hadn't said that. Talk about making yourself look uncool. And I'd sounded like I wasn't keen on seeing him, which I was, of course.

'Oh, well. Just an idea.' Luke shrugged and closed the door behind him. I stopped myself from actually smacking my head with my hands, but I certainly felt like it.

7

Sulphur

The Monday after her birthday, Zoe wasn't at school after all. All the rest of my texts had gone unanswered. I had a bad feeling, low in my gut. After assembly, Kerry followed me to the classroom. 'It looks as if Zoe is having a day off again,' she said.

I nodded. Talking to Kerry felt a little like a betrayal of Zoe, though if you asked me to explain that sensibly, I probably couldn't. 'You sound quite pleased that she's not here,' I said.

Kerry picked at a straggly bit of skin on her thumbnail. 'Maybe. You're nicer when she's not around.'

'That's not true,' I said. 'You just don't like Zoe, that's the problem.'

Kerry bit the skin away. 'She doesn't like me, you mean. That's more like the problem. I've tried hard with her, but she goes on as if she despises me.'

I didn't know what to say.

'Zoe was always quite happy on her own, you know,' Kerry said. 'People just left her alone, because she acted like that was what she wanted. Ever since she first came to school.'

'So?' I wasn't sure where Kerry was going with this.

'You're the only person she's ever taken up with.' Kerry kept picking at the skin on her fingers and chewing it.

I looked away, because it was driving me mad. 'And?'

'You're a lovely person, Anna,' Kerry said.

I made a snorting noise.

Kerry ignored it. 'You're the only one who's ever been nice to me, too. I'm saying that Zoe doesn't need you, she's fine without anyone to hang around with. But she's turning you into someone like her. Kind of, you know, weird. And a bit mean.'

'You've got that all wrong,' I said. I felt sure she had. What I didn't want to say out loud to Kerry was that I wanted, more than anything, to have someone like Zoe as a friend and if anyone thought I was like her I would take it as a massive compliment. And I'd hate to be stuck with Kerry all the time. But I would stay with her for today, because the one thing you didn't want to be in that school was on your own, facing past the groups of girls who would stand and wait for you.

How do they know who to go for? What weird vibe do people like me and Kerry give off? Being with Zoe was like having a bodyguard. And when I was with her, I was a different person, sure – but cooler, I reckoned. Smarter. Not meaner.

After school, I wandered round to Zoe's street. I couldn't help myself. I paced up and down for a few minutes before taking a breath, marching through her gate and knocking at her door. It took an age before I heard some sort of movement coming from inside the house. The door opened a few inches and I saw a sliver of Zoe's mum's face and body. In a throaty voice, she said, 'What?'

'I... I wondered if Zoe is any better?' I asked, swallowing.

'She'll be back at school tomorrow,' rasped her mum, not opening the door even a fraction further.

'I have some homework to pass on to her,' I lied.

Zoe's mum said nothing but stuck a hand out of the door.

'I think I need to explain it to her,' I went on. 'It's complicated.'

'Calling me stupid?' The door was flung wide open. Zoe's mum was wearing a stained dressing gown that clung to her body. She had a strange tremor about her, as if she was shaking with anger.

I looked down at the ground. 'No, I...'

'You can give it to me. Or else Zoe will be back tomorrow. Tell that to the nosy beggars at school.'

I took a step backwards and the door slammed hard.

I walked away, a slight wobble in my legs. I hoped I hadn't made things worse.

But the next morning when I was heading for school I got a text saying: *On way. W8 4 me*.

I lingered near the entrance to The Cut until she arrived. I wanted to give her a hug, but I didn't – I couldn't tell what mood she was in. 'Still here,' she said, with half a smile. 'My mother nearly slaughtered me, though. Next time she catches me, I want you to know I bequeath you all my worldly goods. Because she will definitely finish me off.'

I laughed. 'What happened then?'

Zoe's eyes glowered. 'I'll tell you what happened. That moron Kerry went to my house and told my mother I was off to a concert. Can you believe it?'

'I can believe it, yes. She owned up. She said she was worried about us.'

Zoe made a choking noise. 'Yeah, right.'

I took a breath. 'She's really sorry. She just didn't think it through.'

Zoe stopped walking. I turned and looked at her. 'What?'

'You know what. We've put up with Kerry long enough. We have to get it into her thick head that she's no longer welcome.'

I didn't respond to this. Instead I took Zoe's arm. 'Come on, we'll be late.' We hurried through The Cut, which was even gloomier than usual in the morning fog.

By the time we got to school I just had time to rush into the girls' toilets to try to smooth down the frizzy mess that was my hair, thanks to the damp weather. Zoe's hair still looked angel-straight. When we walked into the classroom, though and Kerry gave us a wave, Zoe strode past as if she wasn't there.

At break time, Kerry rushed over to us, as we shoved our books into our bags. Zoe turned her back. If Kerry spoke, Zoe talked over her, to me, as if Kerry wasn't there. I had no idea what to do. I frowned at Zoe, trying to say something with my eyes. After a few minutes, Kerry tapped Zoe on the shoulder. Zoe whirled round so fast I half-expected her to punch Kerry in the jaw.

'Don't you touch me!' she shouted at her.

Some girls stopped talking and glanced around. An unexpected fight – with words or fists – was always worth watching.

Kerry was shaking, but she stood her ground. 'I just wanted to say I'm really sorry. I didn't mean to get you into trouble.'

Zoe's face went whiter than usual. 'Trouble?' She gave an icy little laugh. 'You have absolutely no idea, you stupid, stupid... You went to my house at eleven o'clock on a Saturday night and woke up my mother, so that you could tell her that I was somewhere I shouldn't be. And you never meant to cause trouble?'

Kerry started mumbling something I couldn't make out.

Zoe stepped towards her, her sharp-nailed finger pointed in Kerry's face. 'You will never know how much trouble you caused. That's what I get for putting up with you. Well, no more. Get lost, Kerry. Go and find someone else to drive insane. Anna and I have had enough.'

Kerry turned and ran out of the classroom, letting out a sort of a wail as she went.

Some of the girls laughed. Whether they were laughing at Kerry, which they often did anyway, or at Zoe's temper, I didn't know.

A teacher put his head around the classroom door and told everyone to get outside, even though the drizzly mist meant we could hardly see an arms-length in front of us.

I have to admit it, in some ways it was brilliant being with Zoe again, with no Kerry to keep bugging us. Zoe was the way I loved her best, all smart comments and sophisticated jokes. And when she talked about Saturday and the gig, it was as if it had all been the best night ever. For her, all the nasty stuff in the restaurant had been sort of wiped.

But I couldn't really enjoy it properly, because I was being nagged by guilt about Kerry. And I had questions.

'So, Zoe, where'd you disappear to at that gig? One minute you were being mauled by that creepy guy. Next you were gone.'

'In a puff of sulphur,' Zoe grinned. 'Hah.'

'I panicked though. Come on, what were you doing?'

'What do you think I was doing?' Zoe's eyes had a wicked shine to them.

I raised my eyebrows at her. What was she telling me?

'Anyway,' Zoe went on. 'That creepy guy is called Tom and I think he's gorgeous. And he promised he's going to get me some gigs with his band, remember? I'm going to dance for them.'

'Oh,' I said. 'That.'

Later, we walked home together, arms linked. The fog had barely lifted that day but at least Kerry still hadn't come back to pester us. 'Tell me what your mum said, then,' I pressed Zoe.

She shook her head. 'It's too boring. Let's just say she didn't miss the chance to have a good go at me.'

'You never really tell me –'

Zoe waved her hand. 'Don't go on about it. I don't want to even talk about her.'

We got to The Cut and I hesitated at the opening because it was so very fogbound. And I could hear loud voices. I looked at Zoe. 'Should we go in there?'

The sounds got louder. Someone was crying and someone else was shouting. Then I recognised the voices.

'I think that's Kerry,' I said, and without waiting for Zoe I marched into the Cut. I walked as fast as I could, but it was muddy and slippery underfoot. Zoe followed, making loud sighing sounds. Round the first corner, we came across two figures – Kerry and Jodie. Jodie had her arm round Kerry, who was snuffling. When I got closer I saw she was covered in mud.

Jodie glared at us. 'Could've done with you two, five minutes ago,' she said. 'Your friend's been beaten up.'

'What?' I stared at Kerry, who was leaning into Jodie's shoulder and snivelling. 'Who did it, Kerry?'

'It was some girls from your school,' Jodie said. 'I came around the corner and they were laying into her. Calling her a grass or something. They left off when I said I was calling the police. I was just asking her where you two were.'

I reached out to pat Kerry's arm. From the stench, it was obvious she hadn't just been rolled in mud. I drew back my hand. 'It wasn't our fault,' I said, quickly.

Jodie shook her head at us.

'Kerry landed us in big trouble at the weekend,' Zoe said, with a pout. 'But we didn't tell anyone to hurt her.'

'They just use that sort of thing as an excuse,' I said. 'Sorry, Kerry. Are you OK?'

Jodie swore at us. 'Does she look it? I think you should take her home.'

Kerry let out a blubbery moan. 'I don't want to go home like this.'

I looked at Jodie, hoping she had some bright ideas.

67

She closed her eyes and sighed. 'All right, everyone back to mine and we'll get Kerry cleaned up. And you can all sort yourselves out.'

I could tell she thought Zoe and I were in some way to blame.

We trudged to the flats, Kerry limping a little. The lift never smelled too good to start with and Kerry made it worse. Jodie ushered us all into her flat and pointed to the little bathroom. 'Zoe, why don't you put the kettle on and make us some tea? Anna and I can sort Kerry out.'

Zoe frowned, but did as she was told and to be honest I thought she'd got the better deal. I had to help Kerry wash her face and hands, which were grazed as well as caked in filth, and peel off her ripped school tights, avoiding a gashed and bleeding knee. Jodie found an old cloth and started sponging the mud off Kerry's coat.

'I'm sorry,' I said. 'I hope you don't think we wanted this to happen.'

Kerry shook her head, blowing her nose noisily on a handful of Jodie's toilet paper. Zoe put her head around the bathroom door and held out a mug of tea. She wrinkled her nose at the lingering smell. Jodie offered Kerry a pair of her own black tights in a rolled-up ball and we left her to try to squeeze into them, closing the door behind us.

Jodie's almost-empty living room was cold and still had a mouldy smell about it. Zoe stood by the window to stare at the view of the gloomy sky and the city lights shining fuzzily through the mist. 'It looks like someone's tipped out a box of gold chains onto a grey velvet cloth,' she said, cupping her hands around her mug.

'Very poetic,' I said, staying back from the window, tiny shivers zizzing down my legs and fingers. 'It looks like fog and street lights to me.'

'How could you two let those girls get Kerry like that?' Jodie demanded. 'You're supposed to be her friends.'

'Yes, well, you don't know what Kerry did to us,' said Zoe.

'I don't care. She's – she needs looking after. Kerry's not as switched on as you two.'

'Switched on? She's not even plugged in,' Zoe muttered and I smiled. We could hear Kerry fiddling with the bathroom door.

'Why do you even care?' Zoe asked Jodie. 'I know what it is with Anna here. She's a complete sucker. She feels sorry for any old waif and stray. And she fancies Kerry's big brother.'

Was it that obvious, I wondered? But Zoe always had a way of seeing into my head, somehow. She went on: 'But what's Kerry to you?'

Jodie looked out of the huge, bare window, one hand fingering the scar on her cheek. 'I was bullied at school too, I know what it's like. That's all.'

'You just have to learn how to scare them off,' Zoe said, with a tiny shrug of her slim shoulders. 'You never show you're afraid, for one thing.'

'We're not all as cool as you,' Jodie said.

Kerry came into the room. 'Thanks for the tea,' she said. She was looking at Zoe.

'You sorted out now?' Zoe asked.

Kerry nodded.

'We'd better get back,' I said. 'Thanks, Jodie.'

Jodie held open the door. Dave was just coming in, with what smelled like a curry in a plastic bag. 'Back again?' he asked us. We pretended to smile at him.

Jodie held up her hand. 'Take care of Kerry, you two,' she said. She was looking at me.

'Ambushed,' said Zoe, under her breath. I knew what she meant. We'd just been charged with making sure Kerry stayed OK, whether we wanted to or not.

8

Witchcraft

For the next few days, Zoe was flush with cash. She said it was her birthday money, though I wondered why her mum was suddenly so generous and she'd never mentioned any doting aunties or grannies. But if Zoe didn't want to talk about something, she was really good at avoiding it. Those bruises she sometimes had, for example. It was weird because they were never anywhere you could usually see. They were at the top of her arms or on her back, places she usually covered up. I'm sure I was the only person who ever noticed them, because I'd be next to her in the school changing rooms, or sometimes she'd get changed at my house, into stuff her mum wouldn't let her wear. I tried a few times to ask about them. Once she claimed she was always falling over, though I'd never seen her do that when I was with her – in fact, she was much more graceful than I was. Usually, though, she just talked about something else altogether. I didn't want to sound like a parent or a teacher, so I didn't go on about it. Zoe could be really slippery, even when you asked her a direct question. I don't think you could have got her to answer anything she didn't want to, if you'd sat her in a chair with a light in her eyes and tried to torture it out of her.

So when I asked her how much she'd got for her birthday and she said she hadn't counted it yet, I knew she was fibbing. Everyone counts their birthday money, don't they? Usually more than once, just to be sure. But I wasn't the pocket money police, was I? So I let it go.

We went to Dead Bouquet to find things to spend it on. It was the only place we managed to escape Kerry and that was because she did some sort of thing at her church on a Saturday morning and didn't come pestering us until later in the afternoon. Zoe once said that if Kerry followed us into Dead Bouquet she would have to kill herself.

Zoe zoomed in on the bookshelves. I hadn't looked at them all that much, though I'd spotted books about goth bands and bios of dead people, some arty books about Aubrey Beardsley and medieval gothic art. I was expecting her to get something like that. But she showed me some books on witchcraft. They were hardbacked and wrapped in plastic so you couldn't look inside them unless you bought them and they cost a stupid amount of money. One was about starting off in witchcraft and one was called *Soulcraft* and it was about calling on dead people to help get things that you wanted.

'That's really creepy,' I said, but Zoe just laughed. 'I have always wanted to read these,' she said, her eyes shining. 'It's driven me mad that they're all sealed up.'

We went to the little cafe next door and Zoe pulled the books out of their brown paper. 'These books are going to change my life,' she said, using her fingernail to slice through the cellophane. She told me she'd been on a website called *SweetWitchTeen* and it suggested these books for people starting off with 'the craft'. She already started doing something called visualizing, which was imagining something you want and meditating on it. 'I asked for some money to buy books,' she said. 'And.' She held up her purse.

'But you got the money for your birthday,' I said. 'Everyone gets money on their birthday.'

'There's no guarantee of anything in my house,' Zoe said.

'You can't believe all that stuff?' I asked.

Zoe shrugged. 'It's worth a try, isn't it?'

I would've thought it was a joke, if she hadn't just spent so much on the books. 'Magic, though?' I said, screwing my face up. 'Come on, Zoe, you can't think anything like this will actually work?'

Zoe squashed her fruit tea bag down into her mug. 'No one tries it, not properly, because no one believes it. It's not waving wands about. It's more serious than that. Even scientists say you can make things happen by will power. I reckon it will be a good experiment.'

'Whatever,' I said, shaking my head. 'But I wouldn't hold your breath for the results. What're you going to do a spell for, anyway? Lottery numbers? The maths exam questions?'

'I know exactly what I'm going to do,' Zoe said. She twisted her skull ring round and round her middle finger and smirked. 'A vanishing spell.'

'Who's first to disappear? As if I didn't know,' I said, imagining Kerry going up in a blue flash.

But Zoe just said, 'Maybe.' She tucked the book back into its wrapping. 'Better not show them to Kerry anyway. She'll have her priest come and do an exorcism on us.' She gave me a wicked grin. 'Hey, maybe the books will be enough to scare her away altogether. That'd be pretty magic, eh?'

I sighed. 'Don't count on it. We need to wave more than a wand to get rid of Kerry now. I reckon we could throw a bomb at her and she wouldn't budge. I don't know how it happened, but we're stuck with her.'

Zoe clenched her fists and made a strangled sort of noise. And I wondered whether Luke realised the sacrifice I was making just for him.

Later on, I had to meet up with my dad. He was taking me out for lunch. It was his new idea for seeing me, because I wouldn't go to his flat, where his girlfriend lived, and there was a post-nuclear atmosphere when he came to our house. I asked him on the phone if I could bring Zoe along.

'Can I bring Ellie along?' he asked.

'No way,' I said. 'I don't want to have anything to do with her, thanks. I've told you that, hundreds of times.'

'Then it's just us two,' he said.

The only good thing was that when he was with me he flashed the cash a bit. A sign of guilt, according to Mum. So I suggested that we went to the Italian where Luke worked. I had no idea whether he'd be on shift or not, but it was a weekend, so there was a chance.

Turned out Luke was there and he was the one who came over and showed us to a table. I was really glad I'd made a bit of an effort to get ready that morning, even though it was more to impress Zoe than anyone else. My black net dress and jacket might've been a bit too goth for Luke's liking. My dad made his usual comments about

Halloween being still a few months away and I just curled my lip at him, Zoe-style.

Luke gave us the lunch menu and winked at me. My dad clocked it. As soon as Luke left us, Dad leaned back in his seat and folded his arms. 'So, any reason why you chose this place?'

I shrugged. 'We came here last week for Zoe's birthday. I thought it was nice.'

My dad sniffed. 'Bit like eating in a dungeon, if you ask me. Still, I suppose it beats McDonald's.'

We ordered our food. I reckoned Dad was giving Luke the evil eye, and I told him so. He just laughed. 'All dads are like that. They want to protect their little girls from big bad boys, that's all.'

'Protect me?' I took a swig of fizzy water. 'But you don't even live with me anymore. I don't think you get much of a say in what I do now, to be honest.'

Dad closed his eyes for a second. 'All right, Anna. It'd be nice to know when you're going to stop being quite so angry with me.'

I swallowed. I always got a hard lump in my throat when I had to talk to Dad about the divorce. 'Don't expect any sudden changes of heart.'

Dad nodded and picked at the bread Luke had put on the table. 'Fine. I might not get much of a say in your life, for now. But your mum's quite worried about you.'

I blinked. 'How d'you mean?'

'I think she's concerned about this friend of yours – Zoe? The one you went to that concert with.'

'What about her?'

'She thinks she's a bit of a – er – an overpowering influence on you.'

I'd been about to bite into an olive. I turned it round in my fingers and all of a sudden it seemed too oily, too sour to eat. 'You mean you actually talked to Mum? That's a miracle.'

Luke turned up with two big steaming plates of pasta. He said: 'Extra helping for my fave customer.'

I knew I wasn't going to be able to eat it and Dad didn't look like he was hungry any more. I looked at the bowl and said: 'Phew.'

'How are you his favourite customer?' Dad asked.

'I'm not, really,' I said. 'He's my friend's big brother, that's all.' I paused for a minute. 'Not Zoe, another girl. Kerry. I don't think you've met her.'

'Another witch-in-training?' asked Dad.

'Ha, ha. Nope, quite the opposite. Actually, she just sort of follows Zoe and me around and we wish she wouldn't.'

Dad frowned at me. 'What's wrong with her?'

'She's just – we just don't like her very much. She's a bit nerdy and she acts like she's five years old some of the time.'

'Why does she want to hang around with you, then, if you don't get on?'

'She's really thick-skinned, Dad.' I glanced around me to make sure Luke was nowhere in earshot. 'I think we've made it pretty clear we'd rather she wasn't around, but she doesn't take the hint. Probably 'cause she just doesn't have any other mates either. And that school... there are kids who pick on you if you're on your own.'

'Right.' Dad poked at his food with his fork. 'So she has to tag along with you, otherwise she'd be bullied. And alone.'

I nodded. 'What would you do, Dad? To get rid of her?'

'I wouldn't,' said Dad.

'What?'

'I wouldn't get rid of her. It sounds like she's quite lonely. I thought someone like you might have got that.'

I put my fork down. 'Well, I do get that. But why should it be my problem?'

'Because you're a nice person. Well, you used to be. I was always proud of your kind heart. I'm not sure I really like the person you're turning into, though.'

It was a bit like being slapped, having your dad say something like that to you. 'Thanks very much. Shouldn't you be on my side? Isn't that something else dads are supposed to do? You know, along with fending off boys. Oh, and not running off with stupid girlfriends, except you conveniently forgot about that one.' I screwed up my eyes to stop myself crying in front of him. Wasn't it my so-called kind heart that caused the whole Kerry problem, anyway?

Dad put his head in his hands for a moment. Then he looked up. 'All right, you're still raw about what happened with me and your mum. I understand that. But you know, ever since you were a little girl, you found it in you to be fair to people. I was always really proud of that. Your mum says now you hardly talk to her, you spend all your time with that Zoe or else texting or chatting to her over the laptop. You don't even read much anymore and you used to love your books. She says you never wear anything she buys you, only all this whacky stuff that your new friend likes. She's worried, Anna. What happened to you?'

I clenched my fists under the table. 'Bad parenting? A broken home?'

Dad groaned.

And then a weird thing happened. A woman came up to our table and tapped Dad on the shoulder. It was a tall-ish blonde woman, sort of pretty, like a Barbie doll who'd got older and a bit chunkier round the hips. She gave my dad a glossy smile. 'You're still eating! Sorry! I didn't mean to get here quite so early.'

So this was the dreaded Ellie and she was barging in on my dad and me. On purpose, I guessed. Although considering the way she'd barged through our whole family, I suppose this was nothing to her.

'I didn't know you were coming at all.' Dad didn't sound all that pleased.

'Neither did I,' I chipped in.

Dad gave me a warning sort of a look and pulled out a chair for Ellie.

'Not pleased to see me?' Ellie practically batted her lashes at him. I thought I might be sick.

'It's not that. It's just – Anna and I need to have a chat –'

'Anna!' Ellie held out her hand across the table. I just looked at it, as if she was waving a dead fish at me or something. She kept her hand held out for a few seconds too long and then pulled it back when she realised I most definitely wasn't going to take it. She kept her smile on, though. 'It's so nice to meet you. Your dad's always talking about you. He didn't tell me you were so pretty, though.'

'Well, he wouldn't,' I said. 'He's just been saying how he doesn't approve of my clothes or my make-up or my friends. Or just about anything I do.'

I watched as Ellie worked to keep her lips stretched into place. 'I'm sure that's not true,' she said. 'I just know he dotes on you.'

'Wrong,' I said. I dragged my jacket from the back of my chair and started to pull it on. 'He doesn't even like me anymore. Or my friends. He's just said so. Right, Dad? But then I guess that's fair, because, you know what? I don't like the company he keeps either.'

'Sit down, Anna,' Dad said. 'You've hardly eaten anything.' He turned to Ellie. 'Look, could you just leave us alone for another half hour or so? Haven't you got any shopping to do?'

Ellie gave another forced smile, her brow wrinkling. 'No, I haven't.'

'Sure? You usually do.' Dad was being really sharp. I stood there, my jacket half on and half off, glancing from one to the other.

'I could just stay and have a coffee?' She turned to me. 'I could referee. Anna?'

I put my other arm into my sleeve. 'Isn't it a bit late to ask whether I mind you being around? My dad might be stuck with you. But I don't have to be.'

Dad looked as if he couldn't decide which of us he'd like to kill first. I took my chance and strode to the door. I could hear their raised voices behind me and I saw that they were having an almighty row and that other people in the restaurant were staring at them.

Outside, I blinked. My eyes were watery. It was a cloudy afternoon, but it felt bright compared to the inside of the restaurant. I almost stepped out into the road without looking and a car blared its horn at me, making me jump back. I got the next bus home, went in and found Mum sitting watching some corny old film on the TV. I put my arms around her from behind and offered to make her some tea. I told her what had happened with Dad and his girlfriend.

'Trouble in paradise, eh?' She gave a little smile that I probably wasn't meant to see.

9

'Bela Lugosi's Dead'

The next day was even weirder. Zoe called round late in the morning and we went into my bedroom to put some music on.

'So?' she said, sitting on my bed. 'Your dad moved back in yet?'

I stared at her. 'What're you on about?'

Zoe lay back on my bed and propped herself up on one elbow. 'You didn't believe me yesterday, did you? You think I'm nuts, trying these books out. So I've decided. The first big experiment is for you.'

I turned the music down a notch. 'I don't get it. What's my dad got to do with anything?'

Zoe inspected her nails. They were painted black with little silver teardrops on top. 'I could only think of one thing I know you really, really want. And that would be for your mum and dad not to be divorced. Right?'

'It's too late for that, though.'

'Yes and no. The thing that I'm realising is that there is always a way. Your mum and dad got divorced, but they could also get back together, right?'

I half laughed. 'And how's that going to happen?'

'Wicca, Anna. I'm going to make it happen. I started work on it yesterday, while you were out for your lunch with Absent Dad. I got a really good feeling about it. So good I half expected he'd be here with his suitcases when I called round.'

I held out my hands. 'Well, he's not. Although…'

Zoe sat up. 'Although what?' Her eyes gleamed.

I sat down beside her on the bed. 'He did have a right old row with his girlfriend.'

Zoe snapped her fingers in triumph. 'That sounds like a good start to me. I just have to keep working on it.'

Downstairs, the doorbell pinged and Mum answered it. She called up the stairs. 'Anna, Kerry's here.' And we heard Kerry's heavy footsteps making their way towards us. We looked at each other and sighed.

'Isn't that vanishing spell more urgent?' I said.

Kerry had brought leaflets about her church concert and she wanted us to come along. 'I'm singing,' she said. 'And there'll be a party afterwards. I'm really excited about it.'

'Singing, as in, just you, on your own?' I asked.

'No!' Kerry gave a little snort. 'I've got a hopeless voice. I'm just in the choir and I'm right at the back because the minister says I sing flat. And I'm not cute like the little kids.'

Zoe made a shocked face. 'He sounds very supportive, I don't think. I'd be tempted to tell him where to stick his sheet music.'

Kerry gave another giggle. 'I don't mind, really. Though I was really embarrassed when he shouted at me for being out of tune. It was in front of everyone. Some of the others were singing off-key at me all the way home.'

I thought: Kerry really is a kind of a magnet for bullies. Even at her church. How does she do it? Compared to most people, we really were quite nice to her. Most of the time.

Zoe narrowed her eyes. 'Want me to get him for you?'

Kerry went wide-eyed. 'What do you mean?'

'Mr Mean Music-Man,' said Zoe. She waggled her long fingers. 'I'm a practicing witch now, you know. Want me to make something happen to him?'

Kerry shook her head. 'No, stop it. Don't even joke about things like that.'

'Go on. Just a little accident where he sits on his baton or something?'

I sniggered, but Kerry folded her arms. 'You shouldn't say things like that. And you're not really – you know – doing anything stupid? My minister says anything to do with the occult is really, really dangerous.'

Zoe waggled her eyebrows up and down at me. 'It could be, for him. It's priests like that who make me want to sell my soul to the devil. Satan's got to be a better bet, right?'

I remembered that, a while ago, Kerry refused to see the vampire films everyone else was into because her church told her not to. We'd all had a bit of a laugh about it, but Kerry took it all very seriously.

'I said, stop it. I mean it,' Kerry said.

Zoe shrugged. 'Just looking out for you. Some people are so ungrateful.'

'Anyway, will you come to the concert? I can give two tickets away.' Kerry paused. 'I haven't anyone else to invite.'

I groaned inside. Kerry had a great way of pushing my 'guilty' buttons.

'A Nazi choirmaster and you singing flat,' said Zoe. 'It sounds like an unmissable event.'

Kerry didn't seem to absorb sarcasm. It just seemed to bounce back at the giver, without her saying or doing anything. 'Brilliant,' she said. 'What shall we do now? This music's really depressing. Can we put something else on?'

'Got any hymns?' Zoe sneered. Then she suddenly remembered she hadn't finished her homework. 'Better go,' she said. 'That's me busy for the rest of the day, I reckon. I've got a pile of it.' She gave me a little glare. 'What about you, Anna? Got homework?'

I pretended to sigh and gave my forehead a little slap. 'Yeah, I forgot, I have, actually. I'd better get on with it. My mum goes mad if I do it last thing on a Sunday night.'

Kerry got up. 'I always do it as soon as I get home on a Friday,' she said. 'That's what you two should do.' Behind her back, Zoe was silently mimicking her.

I saw both of them to the door and after about ten minutes I got a text from Zoe. *All clear?*

I texted back. Zoe rang the doorbell again and I let her in, giggling and glancing round to make sure Kerry was nowhere to be seen.

We put the music back on, louder this time.

'What is it about Kerry, though?' I asked Zoe. 'Have you noticed? Even her priest picks on her.'

'It's like she wears a sign above her head saying "kick me" and everyone else can see it,' said Zoe.

'If she would just kick someone back one time, it mightn't be so bad for her,' I said.

'She's like a big, dripping, wet puppy,' said Zoe. 'The trouble is, Anna, people could start picking on us too, because we're always with her. She's ruining our street cred. I'm not going to that church-y thing for a million quid.'

'We told her we'd go,' I said. 'We can't let her down. It'd be really mean.'

'I didn't make promises,' said Zoe. 'That was you. I didn't sign anything.'

I gave a mock-pout.

Zoe gritted her teeth. 'I'm wearing a wig and dark glasses and a coat with the collar turned up, then,' she said. 'Anyway, who's to say I'll be able to set foot in a church? After all my dark practices? The priest might take one look at me and hold up his big cross and I might get burned.'

'That's just Dracula, you mad thing,' I said. Zoe could be difficult, but then she would take the mickey out of herself and it would all feel OK.

Over breakfast, Mum showed me a picture in her newspaper of a girl band I used to like, before Zoe got me into the better stuff. I looked at it and shook my head. 'Mum,' I said. 'I haven't liked them for ages.'

Mum said nothing for a moment. She took a gulp from her mug of tea. Then she said: 'Oh. I'm sorry. I forgot. You like all that depressing stuff now, don't you?'

I paused. Mum raked her hands through her messy bed-hair. 'I'll look out for anything with – I don't know – Bauhaus in it.'

'Who?'

'Bauhaus. They had a record, a famous one, when I was at school. It was supposed to be the start of the goth movement. I'll remember it in a minute.'

I looked at her with my mouth a little open. 'Are you just making this up?'

'I am not.' Mum got up and moved her breakfast dishes towards the sink. 'That's going to drive me mad, now. I was a bit older than you are now, when it came out.'

'Was it good?' I was still finding this a strange conversation to be having with my mum first thing in the morning.

'It was awful,' she said. 'I thought it was one of the worst things I'd ever heard. I just can't remember the name of the record.'

'Right.' I started to laugh.

Mum laughed too. 'You search for it. Bauhaus. I bet you can find the video online. I'm surprised your Zoe hasn't heard of it – it's just her sort of thing.'

I went over to her and put my arms around her waist as she stood at the sink washing up. I gave her a little squeeze and went upstairs to get dressed for school. She tried so hard, my mum, that sometimes it made me physically hurt inside.

10

Curse

Maybe something my dad said got to me a bit, but I plagued Zoe to make sure she went to Kerry's church concert. We dashed in just as it was about to start and shuffled onto the end of a pew near the back.

Zoe huddled close to me. 'It's freezing in here,' she hissed. 'And I hate churches. It's the smell. I can't believe you've made me come.'

'It's just incense,' I whispered back. 'I'd've thought you'd love it.'

'It's not the incense. It's... I don't know... old stone. Funeral tears. Judgement.'

I linked her arm and hugged it to me. 'Don't be so melodramatic. Anyway, they'd be great names for some perfumes. Funeral Tears, Old Stone. We should suggest them to Dead Bouquet.'

The church choir shuffled onto the altar. It was just as Kerry had said: the cuter smaller kids at the front and the older kids, including Kerry, at the back. I could see her scanning the church to see if we were there, so I gave her a little wave.

We suffered almost an hour of hymns, with Zoe leaning her head on my shoulder and making fake, quiet snoring noises in my ear. At the end, the minister made a little speech.

'I'd like to thank everyone for supporting us this evening. It's taken a great deal of hard work to get to this standard. We have some talented young singers – and of course, some not so talented, but we include everyone.'

'He means Kerry,' muttered Zoe. 'And I bet she knows it.'

'We believe that it doesn't matter that some here are not able to sing well. We think the important thing is that young people take part and spend their time in this useful way,' the minister went on.

'He shouldn't be going on about it.' Zoe glared at him.

'Not like you to stick up for Kerry,' I murmured.

'Yeah, well.' Zoe looked down and examined her fingers.

'... And I hope that you will all give generously to the collection buckets on your way out.'

Everyone clapped politely and we sprang up to be first out of the door. Kerry was slow to reach us. 'Did you like it?' she asked.

I elbowed Zoe before she could reply. 'Thanks for asking us,' I said, not answering the question. 'Did you have a good time?'

'Sort of. The minister says maybe I shouldn't be a singing part of the choir next time. He says maybe I should just help with the teas or something.'

Zoe coughed. 'What happened to including everyone?'

'Yeah, but I'm spoiling it for the others because I can't keep the tune. He's right, I guess,' Kerry shrugged.

'Very charitable,' sniffed Zoe. 'Let me hex him, go on. I won't even charge you for it.'

I laughed and pushed them both out, avoiding the man who was approaching us with a jingling collection bucket.

I didn't put it past Zoe to put her hand in and take some coins out for herself.

The next day it was bright, but it had been raining, and the sudden sunshine made the pavements glitter as Zoe and I walked. Zoe glanced behind. 'Oh, god, don't look but our Kerry-shaped shadow is on its way. She's trying to catch us up. Shall we run?'

'No, stop it.' I gave Zoe a little push. We stopped at the edge of The Cut to wait for Kerry. She caught up, breathing hard, purplish-red in the cheeks. Her eyes were red and swollen. At first, I thought it was because she'd been running, but then she gave Zoe a push in the shoulder. 'You're evil,' she said. 'I hate you. What did you do to him?'

'Hey!' Zoe was taken aback for a second and then she glared back, brushing her coat as if to get rid of Kerry's touch. 'What the hell are you going on about? Don't push me again, or you'll be sorry.'

'Kerry,' I said. 'What's the matter?'

She started to cry. Zoe groaned and I couldn't really blame her. Kerry was always crying. You couldn't help getting fed up with it.

'What?' I said again, trying not to sound as impatient as I felt.

Between gulps, Kerry said that the minister at her church had had a heart attack and died. It had all happened out of the blue, about an hour after the concert. For once, Zoe was silent.

'Euw,' I said. 'That's awful. I mean, I'm sorry to hear that.'

'And you said you were going to get him,' she went on, sniffing up huge globs of snot and letting her tears soak her face. 'You said you were going to put a curse on him. I hate you.'

Zoe looked at me, wide-eyed, as if someone had smacked her across the head. Then she started to laugh.

'Stop it,' I said, gritting my teeth. 'It's not funny. Kerry's upset.'

Zoe swung her bag over her shoulder, still laughing. 'I never did anything to the daft old crow,' she said. 'Honestly, you're such a big kid. If he had a heart attack, it was because he had a bad heart. That's all. Nothing to do with me.'

I started to pick a tissue out of the little pack Mum always stuffed into my school bag. Then I gave up and just handed Kerry the whole lot.

'But you said you were going to do something to him. You said you were going to get him. You said -'

'Oh, Kerry,' I said. 'Zoe's right. You're just being daft. It's a horrible thing to happen, yeah, but it had nothing to do with her. It's just a silly coincidence, that's all.'

I patted her on the hand. I never really wanted to touch her, for some reason, particularly when she was in tears and all runny and wobbly. It made me feel a bit queasy. 'Come on, let's get going. Try not to think about it, eh?'

Zoe was standing with her arms folded.

'Sorry, Zoe,' Kerry said, wiping her nose. 'I was just so upset. I thought you must've done what you said, you know -'

'Yeah, sure,' said Zoe, turning away and striding ahead of us. I told myself I would keep my arm around Kerry until we got through The Cut and then I could let go. The Cut seemed to go for longer than usual, like someone had added on a couple of extra miles.

When we got to school, Kerry went to wash her face. We waited in the corridor. I grinned at Zoe. 'Well, you had her completely freaked out,' I said, with a little laugh. 'She really thought you'd cursed her mad minister.'

Zoe put her head on one side. 'Thing is, though,' she said in a murmur, 'I did.'

I laughed again. 'Right.'

'No, I really did.' Zoe grasped my wrist. 'I used a picture of him from that church leaflet she gave us. I stuck a compass through it. And I said a curse.'

I raised my hand. 'Don't.'

Zoe's eyes were wide. 'You can't tell anyone.'

'Zoe,' I said, keeping an eye on the door to the girls' toilets in case Kerry came back, 'Just tell me this is a joke, all right?'

The door swung open and Kerry came out. Her face was still a patchwork of blotches.

Zoe just shook her head at me. But after school, she brought the torn church leaflet and showed me where she'd poked the compass into it.

'Look,' I said. 'That's his head. He had a heart attack, right? If it was anything to do with your curse – which it wasn't – he'd have had something wrong with his head, surely?'

Zoe pouted. 'Maybe. It's a bit of a coincidence, though, don't you think?'

'Yep. That's exactly what it is. Nothing else.'

Zoe sighed and scrunched up the leaflet.

'You don't want to have cursed him to death, do you?' I said. 'You don't want it to be your fault?'

Zoe thought about it. 'I'd like to be able to do it if I put my mind to it.'

I shook my head. 'No, you wouldn't. You're just saying that. Promise me you're not sticking pins in pictures of anyone else.'

Zoe smirked. 'Thought you said it had no effect. Just a coincidence, you said.'

'It is. I'm sure it is,' I said. 'But you said you were trying to get my mum and dad back together. And suddenly he's arguing with his lovey-dovey girlfriend, when up to now, she could do no wrong. So come on then. How, exactly, are you doing this?'

Zoe leaned forward. 'You promise you'll be open-minded about this?'

I nodded.

'Remember the book I bought? I've been following it to the letter. It tells you how to call on the spirits of the dead to get them to help you.'

'Help you, how?'

'With things that you need.'

I shivered a bit. 'Go on.'

Zoe paused. 'The trouble is, when you just say it or try to describe it, it sounds completely daft. But when you're doing it, it all makes sense and you can sort of feel it working.'

'Just tell me.'

Stop the World by Ghost Dance was playing in the background. Part of me wanted to switch it off.

'You have to make a pact. You have to turn yourself into someone who's going to communicate with the dead and use their help. You haven't got to be afraid.' Zoe showed me where she'd cut a small X-shape onto the back of her left hand. It was a tiny red weal of a letter on her pale skin. 'Witches' mark,' she said.

'Then what?' I shifted about on the bed, finding it hard to get comfortable in any position.

'And when you've done that, spirits sort of attach themselves to you. You can ask them for help. You can do little rituals and they'll respond.'

'Just like that?' I gave a little laugh. It was too ridiculous. 'Like – like ordering a pizza?'

Zoe pressed her lips together. 'You said you wouldn't laugh.'

I held up my hands. 'Sorry. It just sounds so...'

'I know, I know.' Zoe sighed. 'I think you'd get it, though. If you joined in with me.'

I made a spluttering sort of a sound and shook my head.

'Come in with me, Anna,' Zoe urged. She leaned towards me and grabbed both my hands. 'As soon as I started, I felt really – I don't know – powerful. I've never felt like that in my life, but I do now. And look: if I can get this far, and I don't care about your mum and dad half as much as you do, just think what would happen if we both put our minds to it.'

I stared at her long fingers, her row of silver and pewter rings, her pointed nails. My own fingers, stubby and with half-bitten nails, grasping hers. I looked up at her face. Her eyes were shining as if the moon was behind them.

'Wouldn't it be worth it?' Zoe said, in a breathy voice. 'Wouldn't it be worth trying anything, to get what you want so much? I know I would do it, if it was me.'

I swallowed. Zoe's words made me feel as if it was somehow wrong not to try. It wasn't a bad thing to want, was it – your mum and dad making up with each other? It wasn't like having someone get hurt. It wasn't mean or spiteful. It wasn't greedy, like asking to win the Lottery. It was a good thing to want. A normal thing to want. Me, Mum and Dad, all back together again. Like it was before.

'What would I have to do?'

Zoe squeezed my fingers. 'I needed to ask you if I could bring all my things to yours anyway. I mean my witchcraft stuff. If my mum finds it she'll have a fit and she'll probably throw it out. So we can have the rituals here. And then if we both put our energies into it, let's just see what'll happen.' She gave me a shivery, wide-eyed smile.

'Did you ever do that vanishing spell you were on about?' I asked, grinning at her and rolling off the bed to change the music. Just the words 'spell' and 'witch' sounded daft to me. Childish. Which wasn't like Zoe.

Zoe made a downturned mouth. 'I'm still working on that one.'

There was a tap on the bedroom door. Mum opened it and put her head around. '"Bela Lugosi's Dead,"' she said.

'Who's she?' I asked.

Zoe giggled and so did Mum. 'That's the name of that song I was on about this morning.'

'"Bela Lugosi's Dead". Bauhaus,' said Zoe. 'It's a brilliant track. Have you actually got it?'

Mum smiled at Zoe. 'I said it was your sort of thing. No, I hated it.'

'Did the name just come to you in the middle of selling a house, then?' I asked.

'No,' Mum said. 'It drove me nuts trying to remember and the office internet was down all morning. In the end, I called your dad and asked him. He knew straight away. He even sang it down the phone. If you can call it singing. I was in stitches.' She was really smiling.

When Mum closed the door, Zoe turned to me with a smug sort of face. 'She so still loves your dad,' she said. 'She'd have him back, I bet you.'

I thought about this. Maybe Zoe was right. Maybe there was a chance. And I would be doing it for Mum, not just for me.

I turned the conversation round to ask Zoe if she'd heard any more about the band and joining them on some of their gigs. For days afterwards, she'd talked about Tom at every opportunity and it was obvious she was really keen on him. And she was dying to go back to one of the band's concerts and dance on the stage. But she hadn't mentioned him for a little while now.

She picked at some threads on the cushion on my bed. 'I haven't had a call from Tom,' she said. 'He didn't actually give me his number. At least, I wrote his number down, but it wasn't the right one, I must've got it wrong. He took my mobile number too, but I just wrote it on the back of his hand. I'm guessing he's had a wash since then.'

'Hang on,' I said. 'I've had a brainwave.'

Zoe looked up.

'You are going to love me,' I said, getting up and rummaging in one of my bags.

'I already do,' said Zoe, with a shrug.

'Even more, then,' I said, fishing out from the very bottom of my bag a dog-eared old flyer for the band. I handed it to Zoe. 'Here. It's got a list of some of the band's other dates. You could go to the next one and remind him what a brilliant performer you are.'

Zoe stared at it and a smile spread slowly across her lips. 'Thanks, Anna. You're a star.'

I smiled back and went downstairs to make us a drink and take some biscuits. Mum was doing a word search in her magazine.

'So,' I said, filling the kettle. 'Did Dad have much to say? Apart from singing some ancient song down the phone?'

'It may be ancient,' Mum said, 'but your friend likes it, doesn't she? Yes, we had a bit of a chat. He was quite upset about you falling out with him at the weekend.'

I pouted. 'He was a complete pain. And then his girlfriend turned up. I wasn't very happy about it either.'

Mum passed me a packet of chocolate fingers. 'She wasn't supposed to gatecrash, though. He apologised for that. He wondered if you could give it another go on Saturday.'

I scowled. 'I'll think about it.'

'I'll tell him.'

I looked at Mum in what I hoped was a questioning way.

She shrugged. 'I said I'd ask you and that I'd ring him back tomorrow.'

I spooned chocolate powder into two mugs. 'You're getting on very well all of a sudden.'

Mum chewed the end of her pen. Then she said: 'Yes, we are, I suppose. It mightn't last, of course.'

I carried the mugs upstairs and pushed the bedroom door open with my foot. Zoe was sitting on the chair staring out of the window, apparently at nothing but the grey pavement and the orange glow from the newly-lit street lights.

The next morning, it was raining again as we walked to school. Every day in June was heavy and cold and horrible. On the news, they were predicting a washout summer. Kerry was wearing the sort of big padded coat that I hadn't had since primary school. Zoe kept walking behind her and pulling her hood down. Kerry just kept laughing and pulling it back up, and then Zoe would do it again. We slipped and slithered through The Cut, Kerry putting her foot in a deep puddle that soaked her shoe and trousers.

'Trust you,' said Zoe. 'Clot.'

Kerry shrugged. 'I know, I'm so clumsy. My mum keeps saying that too.'

She wanted to know what was in the big canvas bag Zoe was lugging over her shoulder. It was bulky and kept making little clanking sounds. Zoe kept shifting it about as she carried it.

'It looks really heavy,' Kerry kept saying. 'Go on, what is it?'

'I'm moving house,' said Zoe, with a dark frown on her face. I could tell Kerry was getting on her nerves again.

'No, but really, what is it?'

'Just some books and stuff I'm giving to Anna.'

'What books?' Kerry wasn't letting this go. As usual, she was too dumb to know when she was being really irritating.

'Shut up,' I said. 'They're nothing. Just leave it.'

Kerry slowed up and lagged behind us. Zoe strode ahead. I kept glancing behind. 'Come on, Kerry, get a move on, I'm freezing and I'm soaking wet. I want to get inside.'

'Why won't you tell me what's in the bag?' Kerry's voice was whiney. 'You two are always having secrets from me.'

Zoe stopped dead. Kerry and I were so surprised we stopped walking too. Zoe turned around, slowly. The wind whipped at her hair and rain spat down on her face. She didn't flinch. Then she dropped the bag down onto the ground, where it landed with a wet slap. She bent down, pulled at the zipper and put her hand inside the bag. And when she stood up she was holding a knife.

11

Blade

I jumped and Kerry put her hand over her mouth. Zoe said nothing. She just held the knife up straight, clutching at the black, twisted handle. It had a vicious-looking double-edged blade. The rain was getting heavier, its huge drops soaking Zoe's hair and her black coat. For just a second or two, it looked like a scene from a horror movie. In that moment, which passed in a lightening flash, I half expected Zoe to cut Kerry's throat.

Then we heard the slapping sound of footsteps running through the slushy lane. Zoe shoved the knife back into her bag and snatched it up from the wet ground. She turned away from us and marched out of The Cut, towards school, as a couple clutching their coats and hoods against the weather ran past us in the other direction. Kerry and I followed Zoe, much more slowly because Kerry couldn't seem to help slipping and slithering around and I had to grab her arm a few times to stop her from landing face-first in the mud.

'Why does she have a knife?' Kerry asked in a half-whisper, as we scuttled along.

'I've no idea.' I said.

'But she said she was giving that bag to you,' Kerry argued. 'You must know –'

'No, I honestly don't,' I said, gritting my teeth. 'I'll talk to her, all right? But just don't go on about it or you'll get on her nerves.' And mine, I thought, but didn't say out loud.

Kerry went quiet. After a minute, I added: 'And don't tell anyone else.'

Kerry said nothing.

I elbowed her, quite hard. 'I mean it. Don't tell a soul. You'll get Zoe into a load of trouble. She's only just about forgiven you for dropping her in it with her mum. I wouldn't do it again if I were you.'

'All right, then,' Kerry said, but she paused far too long. I wasn't convinced she meant it.

We ended up late and missing registration. There was every chance we would've got detention. But Kerry told the teacher that she'd made us late, by falling down and getting wet. The teacher had no problem believing that. She waved us away.

'Thanks, Kerry,' I said.

Zoe frowned at me. She didn't see I was trying to keep Kerry on side, in case she felt the urge to blurt out something that would get us all into deep trouble.

Guess who ended up lugging the bag home after school. Zoe was under instructions to go straight home, she said. She handed me the thing – I couldn't believe how much it weighed – and told me to put it somewhere my mum wasn't likely to go. 'You can look in it, obviously, Anna,' Zoe said. 'But no one else, OK?'

'But what is it for?' Kerry started pestering again.

Zoe bared her teeth at her. 'You don't need to know.'

I managed to get the bag upstairs before Mum caught me. I shoved it into the bottom of my wardrobe, and put a pile of clothes on top. When I was sure Mum was busy making something to eat, I closed my bedroom door and went to the wardrobe. I ran my fingers across the bag and found the zipper. For some reason, I found my fingers were trembling and clumsy. All of me felt cold, though the radiator in my room was on its top setting. I put my hands inside the bag, slowly and cautiously. I didn't want to slice my fingers with that knife and I still couldn't understand what Zoe was doing with the thing – or where she'd got it. I put my fingers round something smooth and lifted it out, expecting some kind of ornament. Then I gave a little squeal and dropped it again. It was a skull. Without really meaning to, I took a jump backwards. The skull grinned at me from the floor. I gave a few deep breaths. No. It couldn't be real. I picked it up again, although it was like little zaps of electricity were going through my fingers and the rest of my body. I reckoned it had to be a replica of some kind, although it looked and felt pretty convincing. Good job Zoe hadn't got that thing out of the bag in The Cut this morning. Kerry would probably have wet herself.

I found the knife again and a collection of other stuff, all a bit random, to be honest. I had no idea why I was quite so jittery. Some sticks of incense and a pottery incense burner. Candles, two white and two black. An old-fashioned cup that looked like the sort of thing priests use in churches, made of pewter. I'd seen those things in Dead Bouquet, although I'd never seen Zoe buy one. Some thick, creamy-coloured paper, in a roll, tied with a black ribbon. And there was an old biscuit tin with sticky tape round the lid.

It was really heavy. I gave it a gentle shake, but I couldn't work out what was in there, except that it was something heavy, fairly solid. I started to pick at the tape with my nails and pulled it all off in a satisfying long strip.

I was just prizing the lid open when the bedroom door opened and I jumped, dropping the tin on to the floor, where it fell open with a clatter and suddenly my bedroom floor was covered in soil and dirt. Zoe, who'd just come in, gave a little shriek. 'Careful!'

'What the -?' I asked her. I pointed at all the soil and earth on the carpet. 'Look at this! Why the hell are you carrying a tin of soil around?'

Zoe put her hand over her mouth. 'Sorry, I should've warned you about that.' She bent down and started scooping the soil up and trying to drop it back into the tin.

'Hang on,' I said and ran downstairs to grab the hoover. Mum looked dangerously close to asking questions as I started carrying it upstairs. 'We, er, just spilled some – something,' I mumbled.

I pushed open the bedroom door. 'Here,' I said. 'This will be quicker.'

'No,' Zoe said, her voice a little high-pitched. 'You can't hoover this up. It's special – it's earth from a graveyard.'

'What?'

She looked up at me, her hands grubby from picking up handfuls of soil. For a second or two I just stared at her, my mouth open. Then, I don't know why, I started to laugh. So did Zoe.

'Seriously,' I said. 'Why have I got half a graveyard on my bedroom floor?'

The room smelled of soil. A sad smell.

'Because you're a klutz,' said Zoe, still kneeling and scraping the dirt back into her tin.

I stretched out my leg and nudged her with my toe. 'Why have you got it in the first place, you mad thing?'

'We need it. For summoning spirits and doing rituals.'

I squinted at her. 'Are you serious? Tell me this is a joke.'

Zoe gave me a look that said she wasn't kidding. Then my stomach flipped. 'Oh my god – that skull?'

Zoe made a spluttering noise. 'That's made of resin, stupid. You didn't think it was real?'

'Well, I –'

'And where would I get a real skull from?' Zoe sat back on her heels.

I folded my arms. 'Digging in a graveyard?'

Zoe paused for a second and then we both started to giggle again.

'No, but, Zoe, this soil – it's a bit weird, isn't it? How did you get it?'

'How do you think?' Zoe grinned. 'Digging in a cemetery, like you said. The one round the corner from Scrogg's Field.'

Scrogg's Field was behind the high-rise flats. It was another place no one with any sense went near in the dark.

'How did no one stop you?' I asked.

'They did.' Zoe looked shifty. 'A woman asked me what I was doing. I said I was going to plant a bush on my granny's grave. I said I needed to see what kind of soil it was. She left me alone after that.'

'I can't believe you did that,' I said. 'That took some nerve. If someone had caught me I'd have been mortified.'

'That's why I didn't ask you to come with me,' Zoe said, pressing the lid back down on the tin.

'Right.' I looked at the bag. 'What about all this other stuff?'

'You can get it all online. Pretty cheap, too. Well, most of it is. The chalice was expensive.' The chalice was the fancy cup, she said.

'How did you get the money?'

Zoe looked at her hands and flicked away some dirt. 'I had a birthday, remember?'

I frowned at her. This birthday money seemed to be lasting forever, but Zoe never said who'd actually given her all this cash. I blinked and shook my head: I decided I didn't really want to know.

My mum asked Zoe if she wanted her to walk home with her, just to make sure she was OK. Outside, there was a blustery, bullying wind, and more rain. Zoe wouldn't have it, though. 'It's fine, Mrs Ellis, really. I'm a big girl.'

'I know that. I'd just hate anything to happen to you.' My mum is a bit of a fretter. 'I'm sure your mum would feel the same if Anna was walking home from your house.'

Zoe looked doubtful. 'I'll be fine. I'll text Anna as soon as I get back.'

And she did. I sat with Mum watching a bit of bad TV and after a few minutes my phone bleeped. *Home safe n sound. Tell yr lovely mum.* I held the message up and Mum smiled.

'Is Zoe –' Mum stopped and stared into her mug of tea.

I looked at her. 'What?'

'Is she quite all right?'

I screwed my face up at Mum. 'What do you mean, is she quite all right? What does that mean?'

Mum shook her head. 'I don't really know, Anna. But there's something about that girl. She seems very –' Mum stopped again.

'Very *what*?'

'Sort of sad.'

I made another face. 'I don't think so, Mum. No.'

Mum pressed her lips together. 'It's like she's about to snap. About to break into little bits.'

I put my mug down. 'I don't know what you mean. But I think you're wrong, anyway. Zoe is as tough as anything. It's one of the reasons why I like her.'

Mum shrugged. 'If you say so.'

I kept Mum talking as long as I could. For some reason that I couldn't put into words, I really didn't want to go up to my room. Eventually, though, Mum said she could hardly keep her eyes open and ordered me to go to bed too. I padded up the stairs barefoot and as soon as I went into my room I felt grit under my toes. I remembered I hadn't quite got all that soil off the carpet. I brushed the last of it as best I could into a tiny pile, picked it up in a tissue and threw it into my bin. It made me feel uneasy, even though I knew that it was only a bit of dirt. It surely didn't matter where it had come from.

But lying in bed, I felt a bit like I remembered feeling as a little kid, when I'd been told a spooky story. If something had frightened me, I could never settle afterwards. It was like the telling of it made it real and might make the same thing happen to me. I didn't dare close my eyes. It felt as if there were shadows moving around my room. I kept sitting up and glancing at the wardrobe where Zoe's bag was hidden, as if something was going to jump out of it. I imagined I could hear strange sounds, although my head told me they were only the usual ones, like the heating pipes winding down and Mum's footsteps creaking as she put things away and got ready for bed. A sudden gust of wind sent raindrops smattering across the window pane, like a handful of little stones, and I leapt out of bed and pulled back the curtain. For a second, I thought I saw a shadow at my shoulder and I whipped around with a little gasp. There was no one else in the room, of course. I turned back to the glass and peered at it. All I could see was my own moon-faced reflection in the bedroom window.

12
Parents' Night

A fretful sleep full of unremembered dreams meant I was tired and fuggy-headed again the next morning. Kerry lolloped alongside us as usual and her perkiness was so grating that I felt I was seeing her through Zoe's eyes.

'Is your mum coming to Parents' Night?' Kerry asked.

I groaned. 'Tell me that's not tonight.'

'Yes, of course it is. We had a letter ages ago.'

I glanced at Zoe, who made a murderous, eye-popping face at the back of Kerry's head. 'Rats. I forgot to mention it,' I said. 'My mum'll go mad if she misses it, though.'

'She'll get a text from the school today to remind her,' Kerry said. 'New system. They told us about it in assembly, remember?'

I shrugged. I couldn't remember. 'So Mum will definitely find out? Great. She'll kill me for not reminding her before.' I looked past Kerry at Zoe. 'What about your mum?'

Zoe looked at me as if I was crazy. 'She never comes to these things. I'm glad to say.'

'Lucky you.' Kerry gave a snorty laugh. 'They always tell my parents how I forget things and how useless I am at all the arty subjects and at games. Then I get a lecture about trying harder. I hate it.'

I hadn't been at the school long enough to know what its Parents' Evenings were like, but I could imagine. At my last school, Mum always insisted on going along to them and she went a bit sappy in front of the teachers, as if they were important or scary or something.

'Why doesn't your mum come then?' I asked Zoe.

'Don't ask me why my mum does anything. Or doesn't do anything.' I could tell it was one of those questions that Zoe was not prepared to answer. Kerry pressed her a bit longer, but Zoe was amazing at batting the questions away. She should be a politician, I thought, she's so good at that.

Sure enough, Mum ran in the door at five-thirty and the first thing she said was, 'You could've told me about Parents' Night. I can't make something to eat till we get back.'

'You don't have to go if you don't want to,' I suggested. 'Zoe's mum never bothers, she says.'

'You wish,' Mum said, standing in front of the mirror at the bottom of the stairs and patting powder onto her forehead. 'Anyway, Dad'll be on his way by now.'

'Dad?' I stared at her reflection. 'Dad's coming?' Dad used to leave all this to Mum when they were together.

Mum pulled a lipstick out of her bag. She glanced at it, dropped it back in her bag and rummaged around for a different one. 'I sent him a message just to let him know and he said he'd like to come along. I couldn't see why not.'

'Right.' I was still thinking about this when Dad rang the doorbell. I opened the door and he held up his hands, saying: 'I'm on my own, OK?'

I folded my arms. 'Glad to hear it. But how bad do things have to be if you'd rather be at Parents' Night than out with your girlfriend?'

'Watch it.' Dad gave Mum a smile. 'You look very nice.'

Mum gave him a bit of a smirk back and we got in the car. I was watching them closely. Something had made them call a truce from all the fighting and sniping. Was it because of me? Or was it anything to do with Zoe and her spirits?

We pulled up in the school car park and as we got out of the car, I could hear shouting. A small crowd of kids and parents were huddled close to the main door, watching whatever was causing the row. As we edged closer, I saw Zoe, standing still, her eyes closed as her mum screamed at her. Zoe's mum's words were slurred and almost too loud to make out, but she was yelling something about school, about not being told what was going on, about getting the blame for all Zoe's problems. Some of the kids were sniggering. Dad put an arm around my shoulders and I looked up at him, willing him to do something, to rescue poor Zoe who was as still as a dummy in a shop window, her eyes still screwed shut.

Maybe it was because Zoe was refusing to react or even look at her, but her mum was getting more and more furious. Suddenly she leaned forward and pushed at Zoe, hard in the chest, making her stagger backwards. There was a loud gasp from the little audience. That was when my dad stepped in, pushing his way to the front of the small crowd and taking Zoe's mum by the arm.

'That's enough, now,' he said. 'Let's end the show, shall we?'

Zoe's mum swore at him and tried to shake him off, but she was unsteady on her own feet and he easily steered her away towards a bench, where she sat heavily down. Dad sat with her and started to talk, in his low, calm voice. Mum and I rushed up to Zoe and I put my arms around her.

'Are you all right, love?' Mum asked. Zoe nodded, though I could feel her trembling and her face, next to mine, was burning.

'What happened?' I stroked Zoe's hair.

Zoe shrugged. 'She's just being my mum. That's what she's like. She got a message from school and they said something about poor attendance. She lost her rag.' She paused and sniffed. 'It's nothing I haven't seen before.'

I glared at anyone passing who dared to look twice at us. After a few minutes, my dad came up to Zoe. 'I think your mum's calmed down a bit, but she needs to go home. Can I give you a lift?'

Zoe shook her head. 'The walk will do her good.'

'You're not going home with her?' I looked from Mum to Dad. 'She can't. She pushed Zoe. She might –'

Dad put a hand on my shoulder. 'We can't get too involved, Anna. We have to let Zoe and her mum sort this out now.'

'But –'

'It's fine,' Zoe interrupted. 'Honestly. I'm used to it.' She looked over to her mum. 'I'm going home. Coming?' And she held out a hand.

'We should go in,' Mum said to me. 'We won't get to see your teachers if we don't hurry.'

'Text me,' I called after Zoe as she strolled away, her mum stumbling along behind her. 'I mean it. Let me know you're all right.'

Zoe raised a hand in a kind of salute, but didn't look back.

My school reports were better than expected, which put both Mum and Dad in a good mood and I think seeing Zoe's mum's behaviour made them want to be extra nice to me. Dad even suggested that he'd get us all fish and chips. Suddenly there were three of us round the table, like there used to be. It felt really weird. Good-weird, though. I relaxed a bit when Zoe texted to say her mum was in bed and she was fine and would see me tomorrow.

Dad said he'd stay for a cup of tea and Mum went into the kitchen to put the kettle on. We were in the middle of a chat about some cruddy TV show we'd both been watching when his mobile went off. He glanced at the message and I could tell it was the dreaded Ellie. Wanting to know where he was, I guessed.

Dad just switched it off and put the phone in his pocket. 'Tell her you're where you should be, for a change,' I said. 'With your daughter.'

Dad looked down at the table. 'It's been good tonight, Anna. Let's not spoil it, eh?'

Mum came in with mugs of tea. She could tell there'd been a change in the air. She looked at me and then at Dad. 'Everything all right?'

'His girlfriend's checking up on him,' I said.

Dad shook his head and sighed. I felt all hot inside. That Ellie, spoiling things and coming between us all the time. Couldn't she give us an evening together? I wanted to go to her stupid flat and slap her stupid face.

Dad took a big slurp of tea and winced because it was too hot. He put the mug down and said, 'I'd better go, anyway. I've probably outstayed my welcome.'

'Can't she spend a couple of hours without you?' I said. 'I'm the one who's supposed to be the child, not her.'

Mum put her hand on my shoulder and I shook it off. She and Dad looked at each other for a long moment and then Dad picked up his jacket and made for the door. I heard Mum thanking him for the lift and for the chips.

'Why are you creeping up to him like that?' I found myself saying, when she sat down and picked up the TV remote. 'He runs off with a new girlfriend and he totally breaks your heart. And all he has to do is buy a bag of chips and everything's fine?'

Mum put her arm out, but I wouldn't sit next to her. I stared up at the ceiling, blinking hard.

'No, of course everything's not OK,' Mum said. 'But I'm just sick of fighting.'

I stamped my way up the stairs. I suddenly just wanted to get into bed and hide under the duvet. Thing was, ever since I'd hidden Zoe's bag, my room was seriously giving me the creeps. My own bedroom. I kept thinking I could still feel soil – graveyard dirt – under my feet, but when I checked, the carpet was completely clean. I imagined dark shadows just in the corner of my eye and when I snapped my head round, nothing was there. I got really deep, cold, body shivers that seemed to start on my skin but fill my whole insides with ice. Worst thing was, I knew it had to be my own mad imagination, running away with me. Just because there was a plastic skull and some black candles hidden in my wardrobe. Just because I'd spilled soil on my carpet which was perfectly ordinary soil, except that it came from somewhere bodies were buried. Talk about over-reacting. It's not like I had an actual dead person in my room with me. It just kind of felt like that, even in daylight, but especially at nights when I was trying to get to sleep. It was then, in the small hours after midnight, when I got my strongest sense of things about to go horribly wrong, a nagging pit-of-the-stomach queasiness that wouldn't go away, no matter how much I tried to talk myself out of it.

I was relieved to see Zoe the next morning, though she refused to talk about what happened, other than to say she was 'used to that sort of thing.' I made sure to be by her side all day and when Maxine came up to make a snipey comment about Zoe's mum, I swore at her so fiercely she backed off. I was quite proud of it.

Kerry was a bit odd, though. Kind of sniffy and quiet. That was fine with Zoe, because she just took it as the go-ahead to stop talking to Kerry all together. But that shapeless bad feeling I was carrying round with me all the time had a name, for today: what was the matter with Kerry? I guessed it wasn't because of Zoe's mum – Kerry hadn't even seen the incident and didn't seem interested when I mentioned it. It was more likely to be about the row in The Cut yesterday. Had she told someone something she shouldn't have?

We soon found out. Kerry wasn't around at the end of school. I suggested looking in the girls' cloakrooms for her, but Zoe wouldn't wait.

'If Kerry's not ready then she can't expect us to hang around in this dump a minute longer than we have to,' she said. 'She's probably buttering up some teacher somewhere. Asking if she can tidy their desk for them. Putting her coat over a puddle so they don't get their feet wet. Or something.'

We set off for home without her and it did feel really nice. Like we were free of something. It was cool and a bit damp outside, but there was a scent in the air, like cut grass. We could have so much more of a laugh when it was just the two of us. Zoe was telling me how she planned to conjure up an army of demons in the next maths lesson. And I was telling her how my mum and dad had spent an entire evening together without having a fight.

And in the middle of The Cut, someone stepped out in front of us. We both jumped and stopped short. It was Jodie.

'You gave us a shock,' Zoe said, although it hardly needed saying.

'I need to talk to you two,' Jodie said. She dropped her half-smoked cigarette on the ground and squashed it with her boot, making a short hissing, squelching sound.

'What's up?' Just about everything was making me really anxious at the moment – making my heart thump, giving me shivers.

'I've been talking to your friend,' she said. 'Kerry.'

'What about her?' Zoe asked.

Jodie glanced around. 'What the hell is this about you going around with a knife?'

Zoe's eyes widened. I don't think she'd guessed that Kerry would have to blurt things out to someone.

'We aren't going around with a knife. Not like that,' I said.

We could hear footsteps and stepped to the side to make way for a middle-aged man hurrying through The Cut.

'Can you come to my place?' Jodie said. 'I really want to talk to you. But not here, not with all sorts walking past.'

Zoe shook her head. 'I have to get home.'

'It'll only take five minutes,' Jodie said. 'Come on.' She started striding off and it was clear she expected us to follow her.

I nodded my head at Zoe. 'Let's get it over with.'

Zoe didn't budge for a moment.

'Come on,' I said. 'We need to know what Kerry's told her. And whether she's told anyone else. Like your mum, for instance.'

We trudged after Jodie towards the high-rises and followed her into the reeking lift. It seemed to take forever to rattle its way to the ninth floor.

'Does anyone live right up on the fourteenth floor?' I asked, mainly to break the awkward silence.

Jodie gave a little smile. 'There isn't really a fourteenth floor.'

'There's a fourteen button in the lift,' I said, as the door slid open and we walked out onto the landing. 'And my mum always calls this place the Fourteen Storeys.'

'Yeah, everyone does,' said Jodie, putting the key in her door, which I noticed had a big gash in the wood, like someone had tried to break it down. 'The joke is, there are only thirteen floors. But when they were built, no one wanted to live on the thirteenth floor in case it was unlucky. So they changed the button to fourteen. All the door numbers on the top level start with 1-4.'

Zoe laughed. 'That's stupid.'

'Thing is, it's still unlucky,' Jodie went on, pulling off her boots beside the doorway. The flat smelled of mould and stale fried food, as usual. 'That's where all the suicide cases jump from.'

I made a face. 'Ugh.' I felt those little tremors inside, that I get when I look out of a high window.

Jodie waved at us to sit down on her slightly greasy sofa. 'Right, you two,' she said. 'Is it true?'

Zoe and I glanced at each other. 'That depends what Kerry's been saying,' I said.

Jodie sighed. 'Listen. I'm not an idiot. Kerry's not capable of making things up. She said Zoe pulled a knife out of her school bag the other day and that she might've used it if someone hadn't come along and interrupted. Is that right?'

'No,' I said. 'It's not right. The knife isn't a proper one, is it, Zoe? It's just like – like an ornament. And Kerry kept going on and on about what was in the bag. That was the only reason Zoe got the stupid thing out.'

I looked at Zoe for back-up. 'That's true,' she said, with a little pout, inspecting her nails. 'Kerry shouldn't be going around spreading stupid stories like that.'

'You're lucky she didn't tell anyone else, like a teacher or your mothers,' Jodie said. 'I talked her out of that. I said I'd make you get rid of the thing.'

Zoe stopped picking at the chipped varnish on her nails and looked Jodie in the eyes. 'I've already got rid of it,' she said. 'That's what I was doing in the first place.'

I looked from Zoe to Jodie. *I haven't got rid of it, though*, I thought. *I'm the one with the knife now.*

Jodie raised her barely-there brows. 'That's good,' she said. 'You can still get into plenty of trouble, no matter what kind of knife it is.' She stroked the scar on her face. 'I hate knives.'

I was about to ask her about how she got the scar, when there was the sound of a key in the door and Dave came in with a clanking bag of beer bottles. He put it on the floor and said, 'Hello again, girls.'

He had a way of looking at us, up and down, that made me feel hot and squirmy. As if I was doing something I shouldn't. I couldn't explain it. 'We should go,' I said.

'What have I said?' Dave pretended to be upset.

'Nothing. It's just –'

'Are mummy and daddy waiting? Is it nearly bedtime?'

I pretended to laugh. But now, somehow, I couldn't bring myself to get up and go straight away, even though I really wanted to. Dave was staring at the ladder Zoe always made sure was in her black school tights. At first, I didn't think Zoe had noticed, but she crossed her legs and sort of tucked them back. She knew he was watching. That horrible shame-y feeling washed over me again.

Jodie came to the rescue. 'Shut up, Dave, the girls were about to go anyway. You said we were going out tonight. Go and get changed.'

Dave leaned back in his chair. 'You see the way she pushes me about? Bet you don't treat your boyfriends like that.'

'We haven't got –' I stopped. I didn't want to have this conversation.

'Two lovely girls like you? I don't believe it.' Dave was really leering at us.

I put a hand across my churning stomach.

'Unless you don't want a boyfriend. Are you –?' Dave's mobile burst into a loud blast of music and he pulled it out of his pocket and answered it. He walked out of the room to talk to whoever it was.

Zoe stood up. 'Better get off,' she said.

'Thanks,' I said, to Jodie, and we both scuttled as fast as we could out of the door. I pressed the lift button hard, again and again.

'What were you thanking her for?' Zoe nudged me with her elbow.

'Making sure Kerry didn't drop us in trouble,' I said. 'If she hadn't talked to Jodie, she might have gone to your mum, or school, or anything.'

Zoe turned her lips downwards. 'Jodie was just sticking her nose in. We don't have to answer to her.'

'I noticed you didn't tell her that,' I said as we got into the lift and put our hands across our noses and mouths because of the stench.

She smiled. 'No, because we have to keep her on side. She's the only person we know with her own place to stay.

That might come in handy one day. And she's mates with Geena from Dead Bouquet, remember.'

It felt great to get out into the evening air. We took big gulps of breath and I found myself flapping my arms to shake off the lingering smell from the flats. We laughed and linked arms.

'I could kill Kerry, though,' Zoe said, as we strode through The Cut with soft mud under our feet. 'What did she think she was playing at?'

I shrugged and shivered. We walked fast to get back to the well-lit street. 'I think she's just easily scared.'

Zoe made a huffing sound. 'You know what Kerry is? She's sanctimonious.'

'Big word for a school night,' I said.

'It was on a blog I was reading,' said Zoe. 'She thinks she can tell other people what they should do and how they should behave and she's always being such a good little girl. It makes me sick.'

'I don't think she means it,' I said.

'Don't you get all sanctimonious too,' said Zoe.

'I wouldn't try to be anything I couldn't spell,' I said and we sniggered.

'What're you doing tonight?' Zoe asked.

'Not much, why?'

Under the white street lamp, Zoe's face was pale and tiny strands of her hair, frizzed up in the cold, were lit up. 'Tom's band is playing in a bar in town.'

'They'd never let us in. And my mum will never let me –'

'I'm not talking about going to the gig.' Zoe checked the time on her phone. 'If we get changed and go now, we can catch him before it starts, when they're setting up.' She pulled back her hair into a ponytail, smoothed it down and shook it out again. 'After all, he must be getting desperate by now, after losing my number. He might be pining for me.'

I grinned back at her. 'Yeah, all right. We'd better catch him before he dies of a broken heart.'

On the pavement outside the bar, Zoe fished a pocket mirror from her bag and checked her make-up.

'You look stunning,' I tried to reassure her.

She turned to face me. 'Should I do this? Am I crazy?'

'Of course you should do it.' I sounded more convincing than I felt inside. But I knew that was what she wanted to hear.

She put a head around the door of the bar, then ducked out. 'Let's go around the back. I think they'll be bringing their gear in that way.'

In the pub car park, I recognised the battered old van from the first gig and a couple of the band members were there, heaving drums and speakers out of the it.

'Is Tom around?' Zoe asked one of them, who pointed towards the bar. At that moment Tom strolled out. He was hard to recognise without the make-up. He looked older than I'd remembered, for one thing.

He gave us both a brief nod and turned to the drummer with a sniff. 'Not many in there tonight. Another dead one, by the looks of it.'

I heard Zoe take a deep breath in.

'Hey.' She gave him a smile. 'Maybe you need a good dancer on the set to liven things up a bit.'

Tom turned his head towards her, gave a grunt and looked straight back at the van. He smelled of cigarettes. 'Want a hand taking this in, Mick?'

I felt myself going hot with embarrassment. And anger. I wanted to slap him. I could almost feel Zoe's confusion, thickening and weighing down the air.

'Tom. It's me, Zoe.' She was still smiling but it had an edge to it, of something like desperation.

Tom frowned at her. After a few beats, he said, 'Hey! Zoe! Good to see you!'

He has no idea who she is, I thought. I wanted to run away.

'Zoe the dancer,' she persisted. 'Did you – did you lose my number?'

The drummer cackled. 'It'll be with all the other numbers, sweetheart.'

'Look, er – I have to set up,' Tom mumbled, actually stepping backwards. 'Maybe see you at another gig sometime, eh?'

'Sure.' Zoe raised a hand in a kind of wave, but Tom had already turned away and was striding towards the bar. I put an arm around her shoulder and gently steered her back out to the road.

She turned to look at me, her face flushed and her eyes watery-bright. 'He forgot who I was.'

'Maybe he was just busy,' I said. 'You know. Distracted.'

'Maybe he's a jerk,' she countered.

I smiled. 'That too. You OK?'

She gave me a weak grin. 'I will be. Let's go back to your house and play with knives.'

13

Ritual

Mum was standing right next to the door when I put in my key. She went on at me for being so late and said she had to go out for some sort of evening training session at work.

'I did tell you about it last night.' She shook her head and gave me her mum-style pop-eyed glare. Then she handed me a tenner. 'Here,' she said. 'I haven't had time to cook. You and Zoe can get a takeaway or something.'

'Sure?' I didn't really like taking money from my mum. A year or so ago I wouldn't have thought twice about it, but now I knew she always had to watch what she spent.

'It's fine, I've had a bit of overtime this month,' she said, already halfway out of the door.

Zoe and I raised eyebrows at each other. The house to ourselves. The first thing we did was ring for a Chinese takeaway and we ate it in front of the TV, watching some bad reality programme so that we could laugh at all the losers taking part. Zoe laughed a little too hard. I knew that she was putting up a front. If I mentioned Tom, she waved her hand at me and changed the subject.

We put the cartons and the last bits of food in the kitchen and thumped our way up the stairs to my room, where Zoe drew the curtains and put on some music – Ghost, followed by Black Widow. We set everything up

– the skull, the black candles, the chalice, the knife. A handful of graveyard earth.

The music, with its muffled drum beat and mournful-sounding flutes, got under my skin a bit. It sounded like some sort of medieval funeral. Zoe said she loved it and that we should keep it on to create an atmosphere. Everything seemed to make me extra nervy, though. I kept glancing round, over my shoulder, over Zoe's shoulder, thinking I could see shapes moving about.

Zoe shook her head. 'It's just the candles,' she said. 'They make weird shadows. You get so easily spooked, Anna.'

There was a special ritual that Zoe had worked out. She wrote something on thick parchment-style paper, then rolled it up and put it on the little table with the candles and skull. I wanted to ask her what she'd written down, but I thought it might ruin the mood, so I kept quiet. The incense sticks kept up a steady, thin trickle of scented grey smoke, making the air feel full and fuggy. Zoe anointed both of us with an amber-coloured oil, on the forehead and wrists. It smelled like a church at a service for the dead.

Closing her eyes, Zoe picked up the knife and held it high. The candle light caught its blade and made it gleam. It left Zoe's face shadowed out, but I could see her fingers around the knife handle, glowing as if heat was flowing through them. She drew a circle in the air with the knife. Before I could work out what she was doing, she used the tip of the blade to pierce her index finger and let drops of blood fall on top of the skull, where they trickled blackly across its smooth surface.

Zoe put her hands on top of the skull, her eyes still closed. If she'd hurt herself with that knife, she gave no sign of it. I placed my own hands on top of hers, but I was too afraid to close my eyes. In the background, the music sounded relentless, and it felt as if it was growing louder and the drum was banging along to my own pulse and heartbeat. The flutes made me want to cry. We gripped each other's hands. Our fingers felt death-cold. Mine were trembling, but Zoe's were steady. She was whispering, names and words that I couldn't make out, because the music seemed to be drowning everything out, blocking my ears from the inside.

A thundering, banging noise made us both jump and I let out a scream. Zoe blew out the candles in one breath and rushed to pick everything up, while I leapt up and ran down the stairs to see what the noise was. Someone was hammering at our door.

I pulled it open to see Kerry standing on the step. 'There you are,' she said. 'I've been knocking for ages.'

I stood with my mouth open for a second or two. 'You didn't have to bash the door like that,' I said. 'It sounded like you were trying to break it down.'

'But you weren't answering.'

'We might've been out.'

'But you weren't.'

I sighed. 'What do you want, Kerry?' I said this quite loud, so that Zoe would hear me and would make sure there were no traces of the ritual.

'I've just come to see you. Can I come in?' Kerry took a step towards me and I had to stop myself from swinging the door shut in her face. Instead I took a step backwards and let her walk inside.

'Zoe is just upstairs,' I said. 'Let's, umm, go into the kitchen and make some hot chocolate.'

Kerry followed me into the kitchen. I switched on the light and as it flickered into a bright glare, we both stared around. 'Oh my god,' I whispered.

The place looked as though there'd been a small explosion. The takeaway boxes, plates, knives and forks had been thrown around the room. One plate had smashed and was in pieces on the floor. The kitchen walls were smeared all round with red, like something from a horror film.

'What have you been doing?' asked Kerry, her eyes big and round. 'How have you managed to make all this mess? Won't your mum go completely wild? Mine would kill me.'

I couldn't speak. I couldn't understand it.

I ran out of the kitchen and shouted up the stairs to Zoe. She strolled down slowly, giving me a little nod to tell me that she'd put everything away upstairs. I pushed her into the kitchen. Zoe gaped and swore under her breath.

'Help me,' I said. 'We have to get rid of all this mess before my mum comes home.'

Kerry immediately started picking things up from the floor. 'What time is she back?' she asked, pushing the torn, soggy cardboard from the takeaway boxes into a plastic carrier bag.

'I don't know,' I said, raking my hands through my hair. 'But it can't be long.'

Zoe picked up the broken plate and wrapped the pieces in kitchen roll. 'We need to know how the hell this happened.'

'Yes, what were you two doing?' Kerry demanded.

'It wasn't us,' I said, grabbing the kitchen roll and starting to wipe the walls. The sticky, red smears were sweet and sour sauce, it turned out and it took a few squirts of cleaning spray to get rid of them.

Zoe tried the back door. 'Not locked,' she said. 'Someone must've walked in and done this. Charming.'

A horrible thought struck me and I ran into the living room to see if there was any more damage. But it looked exactly as we'd left it. I took the bags of rubbish out to the bin, squinting around to see if anyone was there. It was dark and deserted.

When I went back inside, Kerry and Zoe were arguing. Kerry said that we must have done the damage ourselves and Zoe was insisting that we didn't.

'How could someone have come in and done all that without you hearing them, though?' Kerry asked. 'Although you didn't hear me knocking at the door for ages. Did you have headphones on or something?'

We didn't answer, because at that point we heard Mum's key in the door. I flicked the kettle on as she put her head round the kitchen door. 'Wow, girls, thank you for cleaning the kitchen,' she said. 'Aren't you good? Sorry I was so long. The bus was really late.'

'Kettle's on,' I said, as brightly as I could, though I was still trembling. Zoe made three hot chocolates and I made my mum a mug of tea and ushered her towards the sofa. 'Sit down and relax,' I told her. 'We'll go upstairs out of your way.'

'You should tell your mum,' Kerry said, far too loudly, on the way up the stairs.

'Tell me what?' I heard Mum call, half-heartedly, from the sofa.

I didn't reply, but Zoe poked Kerry hard in the back.

Upstairs, I closed the bedroom door firmly behind us. The smell of oil and incense was still very strong and Kerry sniffed and wrinkled her nose.

'Don't you dare say anything to anyone about this,' I warned Kerry. 'Not even Jodie, right?'

'But…'

'Just shut up, will you?' Zoe's mouth was a hard line. 'It's all horrible enough without you making things worse.'

Kerry's phone bleeped. She glanced at it and said she had to go home. 'Luke says Mum's looking for me. Shall I take my mug into the kitchen?'

'Leave it here, I'll sort it out.' I didn't want to give Kerry the chance to get into conversation with my mum, so I steered her to the door.

Back upstairs, Zoe and I stared at each other.

'What the hell happened, then?' I asked, dropping onto my bed. 'I didn't know what all that red stuff was on the walls, at first. It was like something from a nightmare.'

'Want my theory?' Zoe raised her carefully black-pencilled eyebrows. 'I reckon it was Kerry.'

I laughed. 'Don't be daft. She's the last person who'd do something like that. She's too – I don't know. Too boring. And good. What was that word you said before?'

'Sanctimonious,' said Zoe. 'But it doesn't mean someone's really good, just that they like to look that way.' She tapped her nails on the little table. 'She could've got in the back door, no problem.'

128

'So could anyone,' I said. 'Isn't it more likely it was some stupid kids? Or – or someone who was high on something and didn't know what they were doing?'

'But if it was someone like that, someone who was off their head,' Zoe said, 'why would they stop at the kitchen? Why didn't they come into the rest of the house and pinch something? Your mobile was on the bench, but they didn't take that.'

I screwed up my eyes. 'I don't know. I don't understand it, especially how we didn't hear it. I think maybe Kerry banging on the front door was what made them run away.'

'Hmmm.' Zoe sat back and folded her arms. 'Funny that Kerry was there and no one else was around.'

I shook my head. 'But why would she do something like that? It doesn't make sense.'

'Kerry doesn't make sense, full stop.'

I gave a little laugh, though nothing really felt very funny just then.

Zoe sat forward again. 'Hey. Good ritual, though. I felt like there was loads of power. Did you feel it?'

'I felt something,' I said. 'I think you'd call it "terrified". So that was you summoning the spirits, or whatever?'

'You must've sensed them,' Zoe said. 'I felt like the all the air was full of – of presence. What did you ask for?'

'Umm.' I didn't want to tell her what I'd been thinking about. 'I – I sort of forgot. It was all so creepy. That music kind of got into my head.'

Zoe burst out laughing. 'You're telling me I woke up the spirits of the dead and you forgot what you wanted to ask them? Anna, you're unbelievable.'

'What did you ask for, then?'

Zoe smiled. 'Bit of a list, actually,' she said. 'But not all for me. I asked for Tom to get what he deserved. I asked about your mum and dad too, because I think they're already responding to that, don't you?'

I nodded. 'Sort of. It's hard to tell with them.'

'Be patient,' Zoe said. 'And I told them I was fed up with Kerry. I said, "who will rid us of this troublesome geek?"'

Zoe was half-quoting something from Shakespeare we'd been doing at school. 'Well, King Henry wished he'd never said that, didn't he?' I said. 'Maybe not the best line to pinch.'

Zoe laughed again. 'Stop worrying. This is already working out for us. Things are happening, aren't they? Look at your mum and dad. We just have to keep communicating with the spirits. It works, this stuff. I've read loads about it online.'

'You don't find it all a bit scary?'

Zoe shook her head. 'Not a bit. You've watched too many dumb films. The spirits are there to help us. And tonight – forget all that stupid stuff with the food. That was just Kerry and we both know she's a bit mad. When we did our ritual, it was magical. Something big will happen now. I know it will.'

14

Luke

The thing was, something big did happen, the very next day. For me, anyway. And it was the thing I'd been thinking about during the ritual, that I didn't want Zoe to know. It was Saturday; both Mum and I were quite late getting up and it turned out we'd run out of milk. Mum was groaning because she's useless without her first cup of tea in the morning. I felt a bit guilty because I knew I'd used up all the milk the previous night, so I offered to go out to the little corner shop a couple of streets away.

I was in the shop clutching my carton of milk, half-reading the covers of some of the magazines on the shelves, when someone tapped me on the shoulder. I jumped and turned to see Luke, standing over me with a big grin. He was wearing a big soft sweater and a really mad woolly hat that looked more like the thing that my gran puts over her teapot. If he hadn't been so cute, he'd have looked like a complete idiot. 'Er – like the hat,' I said, laughing. 'I think.'

Luke pulled it off his head, showing his mussed-up mop of dark hair. 'Forgot I was wearing that,' he said. 'My grandma knitted it and – you know –'

'That's quite sweet,' I said.

Luke pulled a face. I thought, well, Anna, that was a stupid thing to say. I'm sure boys hate being called sweet. Even I hate being called sweet.

'I reckon you'd look better in it than me,' Luke said, reaching out and putting the thing on my head. He pulled it down over my ears. It was really warm and had a sort of smell of him.

'Trying to hide my face?' I said.

'No!' Luke pulled the hat off again. 'That's the last thing I'd want to do.'

'Right.' I shifted from foot to foot. The milk carton was really cold and my fingers were getting a bit numb.

'Anna,' Luke said. 'Er… I don't suppose you want to go out sometime?'

I took a deep breath in. I could feel my whole body getting kind of warm and I was fairly sure I was blushing. 'Umm, yeah, sure,' I said, as casually as I could make myself sound. In my head, though, I was leaping up and down and singing something like the 'Hallelujah Chorus'. 'What do you want to do?'

'Whatever you like,' Luke said. 'I'm off next Thursday night. We could go to the pictures or we could go and get something to eat if you like.'

'Eat?' I said.

'Great. Anywhere but the place I usually work, I'm sick of the sight of it.' Luke gave me a massive smile. He had really kind eyes, I thought. Long eyelashes. 'Shall I call for you?'

I thought for a moment. 'I'll meet you in town,' I suggested.

On the way home, my insides were flipping over and over like someone had entered them in a pancake race. This was the thing I'd been wishing for last night – that Luke would ask me out. And the next morning there he was, just like that. It was too much of a coincidence, I thought. The only trouble was – I didn't much fancy telling my mum. And I also didn't like the idea of telling Zoe.

I hadn't quite worked out how I was going to word it when I met up with Zoe outside Dead Bouquet later that afternoon. I could tell before she said anything that she was in some sort of a bad mood. She was standing outside the shop and I waved at her as I walked up to meet her, but she didn't lift a hand to respond. And when I got right up to her and said 'Hi', she didn't answer, just spun around and clattered down the little steps into the shop. I followed her. 'Something wrong?'

She gave a shrug that was so tiny I almost missed it. I followed her over to the bookshelves and watched as she picked up the first book to hand and started flicking through it.

'What's up, Zoe?'

'Anything to tell me?' she said, not looking up from the pages of the book. Another one about magic, I noticed.

'What do you mean?'

Zoe smacked the book shut and glared at me. 'I really don't like hearing about what my so-called best friend is up to from the likes of Kerry.'

I felt queasy. I hate fighting with people and I couldn't stand to fall out with Zoe. 'What did she say?'

Zoe pursed her lips, as if she could hardly bear to say the words. 'Apparently my best mate and Kerry's mega-geek of a brother are now an item.'

'When did she tell you that?'

'I had the misfortune to run into her on the bus. I had to suffer her all the way into town, which would be bad enough at the best of times, without her going on about you and her horrible relations.'

'I'm sorry,' I said. 'He only asked me out this morning. I was going to tell you this afternoon.'

Zoe gave a snort. 'You do realise Kerry is just about planning your engagement party?'

I breathed out hard. 'Don't be daft. It's just one date, that's all.'

'I thought you had much better taste,' Zoe said. And that was just about all she said to me for another half an hour. I found myself hanging around the shop watching her trying on clothes and scents and chatting to Geena behind the counter, as if I wasn't there at all. I thought about just leaving and going home. But I didn't want to fall out with Zoe. She would be just fine without a friend – after all, she'd been happy enough before I came along – that's what Kerry said. Whereas I'd get lumbered with Kerry and we'd be the geek-girls that everyone laughed at. I was only tough and cool when I had Zoe beside me.

'Come to the cafe with me,' I said.

Zoe shook her head. 'Can't. No cash.'

'Don't be daft, I'll pay.' I could hear the begging note in my own voice. Zoe looked as if she could take it or leave it, but she marched out in the direction of the little cafe next door.

She was wearing a long, black, cape-style coat I hadn't seen before. 'No wonder you've got no money,' I said, as she draped it over the back of her chair. 'Great coat. When did you get it?'

Zoe didn't reply, but picked up the menu card from the table and pretended to read it. As if we didn't know it off by heart. 'I haven't had any lunch, actually,' she said. Her nails were gun-metal grey.

'Get something to eat, then,' I said. 'I've got enough.' That was even though I'd been hoping to use the money to pay half with Luke on Thursday night. I'd worry about that later. Talking Zoe round was the important thing right now.

Zoe chose a smoked salmon bagel and a mint tea. 'I was hoping Kerry had made it all up,' she said. 'I thought you'd laugh when I told you. I didn't think it would be actually true.'

'It'll probably just be the once,' I said. 'We mightn't get on.'

Zoe narrowed her eyes. 'Kerry said you hit it off the first time you met and that he's wanted to ask you out for ages.' She made a gagging noise. 'She's going to love this. It'll be a chance for her to hang around with us even more.'

Zoe was right. Of course. Kerry would use it to claim me for her own.

So when Zoe suggested we do another ritual, I said yes straight away to please her, even though the sessions were freaking me out. We went back home with some new incense sticks and a CD. Zoe found she had a ten-pound note in the bottom of her bag that she didn't know was there. Mum told us Kerry had called round, twice. 'I said you'd be back later. Why don't you give her a ring?'

Zoe sighed.

'Mum,' I said. 'If she calls, would you say we're out? Please?'

'Why?' Mum frowned at me.

'Because – because – oh, Mum, she's a pain in the neck. I can't be bothered with her tonight. Please.'

Mum shook her head at me. 'I'm not happy about that sort of thing. It's not nice and I don't like lying to the poor girl.'

'Let's just go out, then,' Zoe suggested. 'I mean, I know it's raining. But we'll be OK. We could find a bus shelter or somewhere to hang about, couldn't we, Anna?'

Mum rolled her eyes. 'All right. But just this once. I'm not going to make a habit of it. This is something you need to sort out yourself.'

Mum even let Zoe stay for something to eat. And she kept Kerry at the door while we sat in the kitchen with our hands over our mouths, trying not to snigger out loud. It was clear Kerry was being pretty persistent, but in the end, she had to take Mum's word that we weren't there. Mum came back inside and clattered some plates around. 'That was awful. She said she'd seen you coming along the street. I had to persuade her you'd gone straight back out again and I don't think she believed me. I'm not doing that ever again, girls. I felt terrible.'

Once we were sure Kerry wouldn't come back, we told Mum we were going to listen to music in my room. And as soon as I was sure she was sitting in front of her favourite TV programme, we closed the door, drew the curtains and set up our altar. Candles, skull, incense, a handful of graveyard earth. The knife.

'You should offer some of your blood, like I do,' Zoe said.

I shook my head. 'Too squeamish. Remember what I was like when we just talked about blood in biology? I nearly passed out then.'

'It's a couple of drops,' Zoe argued. 'The point is, you're giving something to the spirits to thank them for helping you. It'll take a few seconds. Come on. You have to take this more seriously. We're not messing about here.'

I stared down at the skull, which was a sickly yellow-white in the candle light. It still had a couple of brownish smears of Zoe's blood from the last ritual. I couldn't say to Zoe that actually, I only wanted to mess about. It was the seriousness of the thing that scared the life out of me.

We started the music again, not too loud because I wanted to keep an ear out for Mum. If she opened the door and caught us, she'd have a fit. I held my hand over the skull, as Zoe said her ritual words. It started with her saying some names and calling on the spirits to help her. The names were her dad, she said, and the woman from the grave nearest to where she'd taken the soil. Then she read out more lines that sounded like a sad poem. She'd written it all herself. I had a second or two of sharp pain as Zoe dug the tip of the knife into the tip of my index finger and pressed it gently so that three drops of blood fell down onto the skull. They trickled slowly across it, like dark tears. She did the same to her own finger and the drops of blood fell onto mine. Zoe pushed my clammy hands down onto the cool smoothness of the skull. She placed her hands on top of mine and held them down. Her eyes were closed and her eyelids trembled like black moths on the pale flower of her face.

'Ask for whatever you want, now,' she whispered. 'It will happen.'

The music sighed sadly in the corner of the room. I tried to tell myself I was just imagining the dark shapes moving around in the corner of my vision, and the way the room seemed to be deathly cold. I squeezed my eyes shut and thought about Mum and Dad. I pushed away any thoughts of Luke.

15

Shadows

Mum got engrossed in some film on TV and forgot Zoe was here. She jumped when we came down the stairs at almost midnight.

'Zoe! I thought you'd gone ages ago. I can't send you out on your own at this time of night. I'll walk you back and apologise to your mum.'

'There's no need,' Zoe tried to insist, but Mum wasn't having any of it and steered her out of the back door. I cleaned my teeth, then pushed open the door to my room, flicking the light on as quickly as possible. This was supposed to be my private space, but now I hated to be alone in it. Even in the brightness, I was sure those shadows were moving just out of my line of sight – with nothing there when I turned my head to look. The air in the room still seemed thick with scent; sandalwood, vervain and lavender from the incense and that sweet, waxy smell candles leave behind when you've put them out. And apart from the odd car shushing past outside, there was no sound.

I threw myself into bed and pulled the duvet up around me. I reached for a book. Zoe had lent me *Gormenghast*, because she'd been doing some drawings inspired by it, but I was finding it hard to get into. I settled for some poems we were supposed to read for English. It wasn't long before my eyelids started to feel heavy, so I pushed the book aside and lay down. I drifted off, but dreamed the bed was full of filthy, grey soil, filling up my nose, ears and mouth, suffocating me.

I jumped upright and blinked hard. When you wake up after sleeping under a bright light, your eyes feel sore and your head hurts. It felt like there was no air in the room and I could barely breathe. I pulled my legs up towards me, hugged my knees and started to cry.

At some point in the small hours of the morning, with a pinkish sunrise sending little glowing shafts through the gap in my curtains and with the bedroom light still burning, I slept again, lying on top of the duvet. I only woke up when I heard Mum tapping on the door. I sat up, rubbed my sore eyes and padded to the door.

'You OK?' Mum handed me a mug. 'Your light's been on for ages so I thought you were awake. But you didn't come down.' She glanced at my face. 'You look awful.'

'Thanks.' I rubbed sticky sleep out of my eyes and yawned. 'Did you get Zoe home all right?'

Mum pulled her dressing gown belt a little tighter. 'I got her home,' she said. 'As to whether she's all right –' Mum sighed and shook her head.

'What do you mean?'

'That mother of hers. She'd latched the door and wasn't going to let her in. She made her stand on the doorstep in the rain for ages and just shouted some horrible names at her out of the bedroom window. I thought I was going to have to bring Zoe back for the night.'

Zoe still wouldn't be dragged into talking about her mother, even after the horrible scene at Parents' Night. Most of the time she still dodged the subject of her home life altogether. I kept telling myself she must be handling it – she'd tell me if there was a real problem, right?

'She always looks as if she's going to fall apart, that girl.' Mum clucked and tutted for a few minutes and went down to make me some toast.

As soon as she'd gone, a shudder went down my back, as if someone had dropped an icicle down it. I closed the door and pulled back the duvet again. There was nothing to be seen, apart from a couple of tiny bits of grit that could have come from the soles of my feet at any time. I blinked and rubbed my hands across the bottom sheet. Nothing. I sat down hard on the bed and took some deep breaths, because suddenly I felt light-headed. I thought, I must be going completely mad.

It was a slow, dull Sunday, especially after Zoe texted to say she was grounded for being late home. But around five-ish in the afternoon, my dad turned up at the door. Unexpected. He said he'd just come to see how his little girl was doing.

'You look awful,' Mum said, for the second time that day, but this time to him. 'What's happened? Come on.'

Dad tried to pretend he didn't know what she was talking about, but Mum said when you've been married to someone for sixteen years – even if you've split up – you always know when something's wrong.

And it turned out that he'd had this massive bust-up with Evil Ellie and she'd chucked him out. And it was her flat in the first place, so she had every right to do it.

'Where are you staying?' Mum asked.

Dad turned his coffee cup round and around. 'In the TravelStop near the station.' It was one of those cheap, very basic hotels. He'd been there since last night. Since about an hour after Zoe and I had done our ritual, in fact. What I couldn't understand was why I felt so guilty about that. After all, this was what was supposed to happen. It had to go wrong with Ellie first, in order for Dad to come back to Mum. But Dad looked so tired and sad.

'Could he stay here?' I asked. I gave Mum a cheesy smile.

Mum hesitated, while Dad shook his head and tried to make out he was fine.

'You'd have to kip on the sofa,' she said. 'I don't think it's the most comfortable place to sleep.'

'I don't want to put you to any trouble,' Dad said, but I could tell by his eyes that he was keen on the idea.

'You won't,' Mum said. She folded her arms. 'You get your own food and you do your own washing. That's if you're here that long. She – Ellie – might relent soon.'

Dad hung his head a little. 'Thanks. I don't deserve you.'

'That's true,' I said and cuffed him across the back of the head. Then I ran out into the back yard to text Zoe: *U ll never guess. Dad is here. Evil E threw him out. Last nite!!!*

She pinged back straight away. *Now u believe me?*

I sat up until midnight just chatting with Dad. It made me realise something: I didn't know everything about him, as I'd thought I did. With Mum and Dad, I'd only seen them in 2-D, in terms of what they did for me, when actually they have all this other stuff going on. My dad was interested in things I didn't know about. I'd never have guessed that he'd read some books I like. I had to admit that it was Ellie who'd got him into some of them, though. Also, he knew more than I thought about goth rock bands. I even got him to sing 'Bela Lugosi's Dead' and I totally got why it'd made Mum laugh so much.

The next day, Zoe caught up with me at the edge of The Cut as usual, and when she saw me she ran up and threw her arms around me. We gave each other a tight hug. 'That's amazing, amazing, amazing,' she said, with a little high note in her voice. It was so unlike Zoe to get excited like this, that I couldn't help laughing. 'Tell me he's still with you?' she added.

I nodded. 'Yes. He and Ellie have fallen out big time. He's sleeping on the sofa and he hasn't had a row with Mum yet.' I held up my crossed fingers.

Kerry was lurking behind us. 'What's happened?' she asked.

Zoe and I looked at each other.

'Tell me,' Kerry said, in that grating whine.

Zoe gave me a meaningful glare. I knew I could only tell Kerry half of the story. I explained that my Dad was staying with us because he'd fallen out with his girlfriend. And that I was hoping he'd get back with my mum.

'Oh. Right.' Kerry was nowhere near as excited for me as she should be, I thought. Zoe knew, though, just how big a deal it all was. Zoe understood me.

That wasn't all. Zoe followed Tom's band, Gothic Winter, online and she linked me to a news item on their website. Their van had been in a minor crash – they'd escaped with cuts and bruises but the van was a write-off and it meant they were going to be off the road for a few weeks. There was a picture of Tom with a bandage across his nose. 'An improvement, if you ask me,' I said, making Zoe giggle.

'We did it again, though,' she whispered. 'I asked for payback, because of what he did to me. And look what happened.'

'It could be coincidence again,' I pointed out. 'Mum had the radio news on this morning and there've been a few accidents, because of all the rain.'

'There've been a lot of coincidences since we started doing magic,' Zoe said. It was hard to argue with that.

We had exams at school, because it was almost July and the end of the term. But I couldn't get my head into the zone. I had my dad back at home like I'd wanted and I was about to go out with Luke. On an actual date. Zoe made her disgust about this quite plain. It really didn't help that Kerry wouldn't shut up about it and kept making really embarrassing jokes.

'It's like having a five-year-old kid sister or something,' I grumbled to Zoe in between classrooms. 'Except one that's a good head taller than me.'

Zoe yawned. 'Don't expect any sympathy from me,' she said. 'This is what you get for going out with the prize jerk's brother.'

Zoe's disapproval took some of the shine off my romantic night out. The other issue was whether I should come clean to Mum and Dad about where I was going. The funny thing was, I realised, if it had just been Mum, I'd probably have told her the truth, but Dad being there complicated things just a bit. He'd ask more questions about it than Mum, I knew. And he'd insist on dropping me off and picking me up, and he'd arrive too early, and he'd probably be grumpy with Luke and treat him like he was some kind of crime suspect. It would all just be far too embarrassing.

So I said I was going out with some made-up friend for a birthday meal. I dug out the least gothy clothes I could find, which was a bit of a struggle these days and I ran for the bus with my stomach feeling like a pot of hot, bubbling liquid.

Luke met me in town and we went to a pizza place – a budget one that was part of a chain. He had a 2-for-1 voucher for it and asked if I minded if we used it.

'Course not. Why would I?' I smiled at him.

'Some girls would be ashamed,' he said. 'But I spend most of my money on my travel to college and I give some to my step-mum. I'm not exactly a millionaire.'

I told him I didn't mind a bit. After a little while, I almost forgot to be nervous. Luke was easy to chat to and he made me laugh. He was studying at the sixth form college in town and after his A-levels he was hoping to go to the local university.

'Don't you want to go away?' I asked. It was Zoe's main ambition, to get into a university as far away from home as possible. She hoped for London, but she'd also already checked out other arts courses, all at the other end of the country. We'd talked about going to the same university if we could.

Luke shook his head. 'Not really. Anyway, Kerry needs me.'

'What do you mean?'

'I don't know how to say it, really. She just needs taking care of, sometimes, that's all.'

He'd been looking after his little sister ever since they were much younger, he explained. If anyone picked on her, he tried to sort them out. 'I think maybe she has a – a – syndrome or something. I told my step-mum she should get tested, for maybe dyspraxia, or –'

'What's that?'

'It kind of means you can be a bit clumsy, to put it in its simplest terms. But it's not your fault. Or else, I said, maybe it's Asperger's Syndrome. That's a kind of autism.'

'Oh, yeah. I have heard of that one. I think a boy in my last school had it. Come to think of it, he was really smart at lessons too, but...' I tried to find a tactful way of saying that he didn't have too many friends.

'Anyway, my stepmum wouldn't have it. She went mad just at the suggestion. So, I read up about it when I can and I try to think of ways to make things easier for Kerry. I couldn't just go off and leave her though. She's too... she's such an easy target.' It all made me sort of wish I had a big brother, even though I'd never wanted one before. It must be great to have someone looking out for you like that. But would a big brother be able to drive away the bad dreams I had almost every night? Maybe not.

It also made me a bit more shame-faced about the way we sometimes treated Kerry. Most of the time, she acted like she didn't notice that she got on our nerves. If one of us – usually Zoe – had a go at her or laughed at her, she didn't fight back. She hardly ever complained about the times we deliberately left her behind, or that we did as much as we could without her, especially out of school. But maybe she noticed more than we thought. Maybe she confided it to Luke. I felt like someone was wringing my insides, twisting my gut.

In the end, I said: 'Look, Zoe is not mad on Kerry, you know. So sometimes we don't ask her along to things. It's just –'

'I know,' Luke said. 'Kerry doesn't always realise what's going on, but I do. And yeah, she can be hard work. But she can't help it, most of the time. And you know what? At least she's got a friend in you. That makes me feel better.'

'Right.' I hoped in the low light of the restaurant he couldn't see me blush. I cast around for a way of changing the subject and asked him what bands he liked.

After that, don't ask me where the next couple of hours disappeared to. We talked about bands: he wasn't keen on the goth scene, but I reckoned I could get into some of the music he liked. We talked about books and films and TV. I could've chatted to him all night and it wouldn't have felt too long. I couldn't believe it when it was time to get the last bus home.

Luke walked me to the end of my street. 'It's been really nice,' I said, hoping I didn't sound too childish.

'Can we do it again, then?' Luke asked. I nodded. He leaned down and kissed me lightly on the lips. I tried to kiss him back and our teeth bumped awkwardly. And then something happened and it was like our lips sort of melted together and the kissing felt as natural as anything.

16

Demolition

The almost never-ending rain in the first weeks of July meant that school trips, sports days and an end-of-term barbeque all got cancelled. We dragged listlessly into the summer holidays. Neither Zoe nor I were going away anywhere during the break, as neither of our families had any spare money and soon we were bored out of our heads. Dad went off to London on some training course and to be honest, I was quite pleased to see him go. I'd forgotten how annoying it was to have him follow me and Mum round the house switching off lights and things to save on the bills. And he was the reason I still hadn't told Mum I was going out with Luke, because I knew he'd be difficult about it.

Zoe was doing rituals every other day and I still kept having bad dreams. Almost every night, I woke up in tears, imagining a bed full of graveyard earth, or that I was trapped in a coffin and couldn't breathe. One time I was sure I was covered in blood and I ran out to the bathroom to find it was only sweat.

It was worse than bad dreams, though. Sometimes, it was more like a kind of hallucination. I knew I wasn't asleep, but I could feel that soil and mud all around me as I lay down. I swear I could feel cold, waxy fingers pressing my eyes closed, clamping my mouth in case I screamed. I felt stale breath on my face and insects crawling through my hair. But if I leapt up and slammed the light on, nothing was there and I would find myself glaring around an empty room, panting, my heart pummelling my ribs.

Mum tried to get me to go to the doctor about not sleeping properly, but I didn't want to. I could hardly tell the GP that I had a bedroom stuffed with tools for witchcraft. He'd surely have me locked away or something.

After a couple of weeks of dull summer holidays, Zoe's mood was sour. She hated me spending any time with Luke and I couldn't cope with all her nasty jokes and comments, so I kept the dates to a minimum. Plus, I felt guilty about the way she'd been treated by Tom, so it felt wrong to say anything about boyfriends at all.

Soon the rituals happened every day. Zoe seemed to feel better after them. The cuts on our fingers where we'd nicked them, to drop blood on the skull as an offering to the spirits, were getting scabby and sore.

One afternoon, when the rain beat on the windows and it was so dark and cold I had my dressing gown on over my clothes, Zoe decided we should cut our arms instead, a little bit, and I was insisting on putting a plaster on mine because I didn't want Mum asking questions.

Just then there was a ring at the doorbell and we both jumped and giggled. 'Who's that?' I groaned, hoping Mum hadn't sent some friend round to check on us while she was out.

Zoe went into Mum's room, which was at the front of the house, and leaned out the window. She winced. 'Who do you think?' she said and I realised Kerry had spotted her, because she gave a half-wave and turned back to me, rolling her eyes upwards. We should have guessed it would be Kerry – if we had, we could've hidden in my room and not answered the door.

'So much for bringing us something good,' I said to Zoe, as we headed down the stairs. 'The spirits sent us Kerry.' 'Oh, dear goddess, what did we do wrong?' Zoe smirked and we shrugged at each other and opened the door.

There she was on the doorstep, looking like she'd found all her clothes in a skip as usual and grinning from ear to ear. 'What you up to?' Kerry asked. She wrinkled her nose. 'What's that smell?'

'Nothing,' I said, hoping that would answer both her questions.

'Good!' said Kerry, bouncing up and down on her toes. 'Guess what? I've just seen Jodie and Dave. They're having a party tonight at their flat. They said we can come.'

Zoe and I gave each other a look. Now this was more like it.

'What time?' Zoe asked.

'They said from six, but,' Kerry glanced around and giggled, 'it's going to go on all night. He said it was a – oh, no, I've forgotten –a demonstration party. Or something like that. Can't remember. Dave said bring a bottle, but Jodie said we couldn't be expected to buy drink, so she said bring crisps or something.' She held up a rustling carrier bag.

Zoe frowned. 'I've got no money.'

Kerry bounced up and down again. 'No problem,' she said. 'I've got loads in here. I had some cash left from the last time my aunty Eileen was here. My mum doesn't exactly know, though.' She gave us a goofy smile. This was Kerry's idea of being really, really bad.

I glanced at my watch. It was almost four o'clock. 'Right, let's go and start getting ready. We'll tell our mums we're going to Emma Wood's house.'

Kerry started to follow us up the stairs. 'Who's Emma Wood?'

'She's a girl at school and she lives on the new housing estate.'

'I don't know her,' Kerry said, as we went into my room.

'That's 'cause she doesn't exist, you dumbo,' said Zoe. 'Emma Wood is someone we made up ages ago. That's where we always say we're going, when we don't want to say where we're really going. Get it?'

'Ohhh.' Kerry flung herself down on my bed. 'What *is* that smell?'

'We said, nothing,' said Zoe, shaking her head at Kerry.

'It's not – marijuana, is it?' Kerry looked at us with an open mouth. We'd had drugs education at school before the holidays. Zoe and I collapsed with laughter.

'It's an incense stick, Kerry,' I said. 'What are you like?'

I knew Zoe was thinking the same as me, that this would be so much better if we didn't have Kerry tagging along with us. But hey – after two dead weeks of nothing, this was an adult party at a mate's flat. Cool, cool, cool.

Of course we couldn't find anything to wear and soon we had all the contents of my drawers and wardrobe scattered all over the bed. Zoe painted Kerry's nails and put some mascara on her, although she made us promise we'd take it all off before she went home. Zoe and I were about the same size and so eventually we found some T-shirts that would just about do.

'What happened to your back?' Kerry blurted out, as Zoe was changing her top. There were a few purple bruises spoiling her smooth skin. Zoe pretended she hadn't heard.

'Hey, Zoe. I said, what happened to your back? It's all bruised,' Kerry persisted, even though I gave her a glare that was meant to say 'shut up.'

'Nothing,' Zoe muttered.

'But it's all horrible marks,' Kerry chirped on like a silly bird. 'Have you had a fall?'

'That'll be it,' Zoe said.

I tried to catch Kerry's eye and gave a tiny shake of my head. How had she not worked out by now that this was something Zoe never, ever talked about? Fortunately, Kerry got distracted by a poster on my wall and started rabbiting on about that. She really was like a baby sometimes. I tried to remember what Luke said – she couldn't really help it – but it was hard.

Then we did each other's make up. Zoe was great at that. She did brilliant eye-liner, bright purple for her, dark green for me, flicked out at the corners of our eyes, and the sort of shiny eye colours that we would buy in moments of madness but never usually got the chance to wear.

When my mum came home from work, we told her we were all going for a pizza with Emma Wood. She even gave me some money, which made me feel a bit guilty but I took it anyway. Zoe phoned her mum from our house. Then we set off.

The rain had stopped. The air was thick and warm and full of promises. Some trees or bushes were giving off a strong, heady scent. My insides were tingling, as if something big was about to happen. I knew without asking that Zoe was feeling the same. We kept catching each other's eyes and grinning. The summer holidays were long and eventless, but this might make up for it. It would give us something to talk about later, back at school, when the other girls were ear-wigging.

'I'm a bit scared, are you?' Kerry suddenly stopped walking. 'If I get found out I'll be in so much trouble.'

Zoe shrugged. 'Don't come then.'

Kerry opened her mouth and closed it again. Then she said: 'No, I want to come. It's just – I'm a bit nervous.'

'More than happy to go without you,' Zoe said, turning away and striding forward.

I looked at her, then at Kerry, who'd gone red in the face. I went back and put my hand on her arm, touching as lightly as I could get away with.

'Come on, Kerry. Zoe doesn't mean that. We wouldn't even know about the party if Jodie hadn't invited you. You won't get in trouble, I promise. It'll be fun.'

Zoe was still pacing ahead. I took a deep breath, linked arms with Kerry and marched her on. She looked at me as if I'd just saved her life.

'Hey,' I said, trying to get Zoe back. 'What do you think they meant by a demonstration party, anyway? Is it like an anti-government demonstration or something?'

'I can't see it,' said Zoe. 'It's probably one of those things where people try to sell you stuff. Make up and things. One of my mum's friends used to do it. Mum got annoyed

154

'cause she felt like she had to buy something, even when she didn't want to. Maybe Jodie is trying to earn extra money.'

'Hope it's not that,' I said.

'Hey, maybe it's one of those ones where they show you sexy underwear and stuff.' Zoe gave Kerry a sly grin.

Kerry blushed again. 'Oh, no, you don't really think –'

'No, I don't,' I said. 'Jodie wouldn't be up for it. 'Specially not with that Dave around. Imagine him in a – a – bra and suspenders or something.'

That made Zoe and Kerry laugh and the heavy air lifted, just a little.

As soon as we reached the stairs of the high-rises, we could hear the pounding of music. We ran up the concrete steps, Zoe covering her nose and mouth, until we got to the ninth level. Jodie's door was open, so we gave a quick knock and went in, Zoe waving her hands about because of the smell of cigarette smoke. There were a few people we didn't know sitting on the floor, but we found Jodie in her tiny kitchen. She grinned at us. 'Hey, you came. I thought you might be sick of your own company by now.'

She took the crisps and put them into plastic bowls. Kerry started eating some straight away, in big handfuls.

'Welcome to the demolition party,' Jodie said.

'Demolition! Not demonstration,' Zoe said, scorn in her voice, shaking her head in Kerry's direction. 'We thought you were going to try and sell us some knickers.'

Jodie sniggered at the thought. 'The flats are being knocked down in a couple of months' time,' she said.

'Loads of people have already moved out. We'll have to go too. In a few weeks, maybe. So we thought we'd have a big party. I mean, it doesn't matter if the place gets completely trashed, does it?'

Kerry giggled and took a huge slurp of whatever Jodie had put in her plastic glass. She coughed and wiped her eyes. 'What's that?'

'It's only cider,' Jodie told her. Zoe gulped her drink down fast.

I took a sip and tried not to wince. 'Kerry,' I said. 'Don't have any more of that, eh? If you don't want to get into trouble, then it's probably not a good idea to go home drunk.'

'We're not her childminders,' said Zoe, pouring herself another drink from the huge bottle on the kitchen bench.

It was like something very bad had got into Zoe. I poured Kerry some of the coke she'd brought along with the crisps.

'Are you not drinking that?' Zoe asked, nodding at my cider.

'Sorry,' I said, making sure Jodie didn't hear. 'It tastes like apple-flavoured wee to me.'

Zoe took my glass and drank that too.

We wandered into the smoky living room and danced to a few tracks, Zoe looking like a kind of wild, bad fairy and Kerry like someone who couldn't hear the music at all.

Gulping at another glass of something — wine, maybe — Zoe pushed at a window, although it wouldn't open very far because of some sort of lock contraption.

'You know why that's there?' said Dave's voice, behind us. 'To stop people chucking themselves out.'

'What, killing themselves?' Kerry was goggle-eyed.

'Well, that would probably be the result if you fell nine storeys,' said Zoe. She gave Kerry a little push. 'Why don't you give it a go and see?'

'These flats have the worst suicide rate in the city,' said Dave, like it was something to be proud of.

'I can't believe you have to move,' Zoe said, gazing out at the view, which still gave me vertigo. 'This fantastic cityscape. I could look at it all night.'

'Yeah, it's a really desirable residence. Damp, mould, asbestos. We've got it all.' Dave grinned at us. 'Don't you girls look nice tonight?'

Kerry went all stupid and giggly again. Zoe cast around the room. 'Are those paint cans?'

'Certainly are. The place is about to be flattened. We thought some people might want to write some last words on the walls.'

Zoe picked up a spray can and shook it. She started spray painting 'Zoe' on the living room wall, in vampire red.

'Go for it, babe,' said Dave, a leer on his face.

Zoe picked up another can and started embellishing the letters in a vivid turquoise blue. Spatters went in every direction and the chemical smell of the paint mingled with the booze and the cigarette smoke. She started on 'Anna'.

Kerry watched with a stupid grin on her face, clutching her drink. 'Do Kerry,' she said.

'Write your own things,' said Zoe.

I looked at Kerry, who was still smiling, just not quite as widely. I picked up a can too. 'Come on,' I said, 'I can do "Kerry". Just underneath the "Anna". That'll look good.' I started spraying. Meanwhile Zoe was already turning her painting into a work of art. She had cider in one hand and spray paint in the other. Some of the cider slopped onto the floor. 'Whoops,' Zoe said.

I tried to make the painting look as good as Zoe's, but it was shaky and the shape of the letters wasn't right. By now, a few others were joining in, spraying paint on the floor and the windows as well as the walls. Kerry was just watching, an anxious smile on her face. The music got louder.

Zoe turned to me. She had the black spray can in her hand. 'Nope,' she said, looking the lettering up and down. 'We are Zoe and Anna. Not Kerry. That name doesn't belong with ours.'

She shook the can hard up and down. Then she started spraying black lines all over Kerry's name. She kept going until the can ran out of paint. She picked up another can and carried on.

'Why are you doing this?' I asked, trying to keep a little distance between myself and the paint can. 'Why does it matter?'

'If you don't know,' Zoe said, her teeth clenched, still aiming the can like a weapon, 'then I can't tell you.'

I suddenly thought: I hate it here. I hate the smell and the mess and the way Zoe is being. Someone turned the music up again and it felt like it was going through my brain and into my bones and skin. I turned around to see that Kerry was sitting on the floor, deep in conversation with Dave.

'Hey,' I said to Zoe. 'That man seriously gives me the creeps.' She ignored me.

I went over and sat beside them. 'Kerry, I'm thinking we should get going now.'

'School tomorrow, is it, little girls?' Dave poured some of his drink into Kerry's glass. 'Got homework to do?'

Kerry giggled helplessly. Why did she find him so funny? I looked back at Zoe, who'd turned my paintwork into a huge blob of dripping black. She'd stopped spraying and was taking big, desperate gulps from her glass.

Just then Jodie turned up. She gave Dave a look I didn't understand, but it made me feel like I shouldn't be there. I held out my hand to Kerry and hauled her up.

'Come on,' I told her. 'We honestly need to go.'

I tapped Zoe on the shoulder. She was shaking an empty paint can up and down and saying: 'It's stopped working. It's stopped working.'

'It's empty, you idiot.'

Kerry was still doing that silly giggle and Zoe looked at her murderously.

I linked both their arms and started trying to frog-march them both towards the open door. More people were just arriving, clanking carrier bags full of drink. One horrible bloke stroked my hair on the way out and said: 'Hey, beautiful, don't go so soon.' I shuddered and tried to hurry the others up, which wasn't easy – Kerry was in no hurry and Zoe kept bumping into things.

Outside, the air was still warm. Pink clouds sat, unmoving, in the sky. Zoe was pale and sweaty. She'd got my T-shirt covered in spatters of paint. 'Right,' I said. 'We need to walk around for a bit. We all reek of fag smoke and cider and stuff.'

'I feel sick,' said Zoe and suddenly she did look a very odd colour.

'That'll be all that booze, you muppet,' I said. 'It looked like the sort of stuff people who live on park benches drink. I don't know why –'

Zoe lurched away from me and held her hand over her mouth.

'If anyone sees us like this, we'll be in deep you-know-what,' I said, more to Kerry than Zoe.

She nodded. 'Shall I go back and get Jodie?'

I hesitated. 'If you like.'

A few minutes later, Jodie was helping Zoe back into the lift. 'I don't think she should go back to your flat, though,' I said, trying to think straight. 'It's too – you know – it's quite smoky. And she might end up getting more to drink.'

'I've an idea,' Jodie said. 'I've got a key to one of the empty flats. My mates moved out a couple of weeks ago. Zoe can crash there until she feels a bit better.'

Jodie could be so nice, sometimes, I thought. Even if she was a bit strange and her boyfriend was a total creep.

We found ourselves on the very top floor of the flats, with me clinging on to Zoe, trying to keep her upright and walking and telling her to hang on for a few more minutes. When Kerry tried to help, Zoe pulled away.

We let ourselves into Flat 1413. It was chilly and smelled damp and mouldy, like Jodie's place. There were no carpets or anything on the floor, just a sort of a dark brown tile. It'll be easy to clean if Zoe is sick, I thought.

Zoe leant against the wall, then slumped down onto her backside. 'Ouch.' She sniggered. Then she leaned forward and threw up.

Kerry clapped a hand to her mouth. Usually, just the thought of someone being sick makes me retch too, but maybe because it was Zoe, I was able to hold her hair out of her face and keep my other arm around her until it was all out of her system.

'Kerry, job for you,' I said. I handed her several tabs of minty chewing gum, warm from my pocket. 'First. Eat this. Then go home and find a couple of clean tops we can borrow and get them back here as soon as you can. Oh, and some body spray or deodorant or something. And – and – a bottle of water, if you can get it. Try not to get spotted. Go on, don't just stare at me like that!'

Kerry darted off. To give her her due, she was pretty quick, although it was a good job Zoe was in no fit state to comment on the T-shirts she brought us. For one thing, Kerry was much bigger than either of us and I swear one of them had some sort of teddy bear print on it, but at least the clothes didn't smell of cigarettes or sick. She'd brought a big bottle of water, some of which I persuaded Zoe to drink. Then I helped her change into Kerry's clean top before putting one on myself. I looked at the T-shirts we'd been wearing. 'These are pretty well ruined,' I said. 'We might as well chuck them away.' I rolled them up and shoved them into a corner. I fanned Zoe's face with my hands.

'What the hell are you doing?' she said, batting me away.

'Feeling any better?' I asked. She just groaned.

'Kerry. Well done, girl,' I said and squeezed her arm. 'You might have just saved our skins tonight. If we'd gone back home in that state we may not have lived to see the end of the summer holidays.'

Kerry beamed. She tried the tap in the bathroom and it worked. 'I thought the water would be off,' she said. 'Look, it's working.'

I soaked my other top with cold water and I cleaned up Zoe's face and hair.

'Let's risk going back now,' I said. 'And try to get up the stairs and cleaned up properly before we have to get into conversations with our mums.'

Somehow, we made it. Kerry was a bit more savvy than I'd thought, after all. I flung myself in the shower, got changed and shoved my clothes in the washing machine, which of course made Mum suspicious when she came downstairs.

'All right, what's going on? Usually I have to prise your clothes out of your room when they're about to walk down the stairs themselves.'

'That doesn't make sense. If they were about to walk down themselves, why would you have to –'

'Don't get smart. What did you not want me to see?'

I looked at the floor. 'I got pasta sauce down my T-shirt. Sorry.'

My mum turned on her domestic-goddess act and started telling me that I was supposed to steep it in cold water first and that the stain would probably never come out now. I just acted dumb and kept saying sorry. I kept thinking I could still smell cigarettes and cider, but I must have just imagined it, because if there was even a trace of them Mum would have picked it up like a tracker dog.

I didn't sleep well again, of course. Being exhausted seemed to count for nothing on these long nights. There was a faint smell lingering in the room from the afternoon's ritual. I supposed it had to be the incense, gone a bit stale. But it reminded me of sulphur. My eyelids felt like someone had pushed stones onto them and I let them close.

Something scratched at my face and I leaped up with a shriek. I scrabbled at the wall for the light switch. The light came on for a split second before the bulb blew with a loud snap, leaving me blinking in the black dark again. Panting, with a thumping heart, I fumbled on my bedside table for my phone and in my panic I knocked it so it slid onto the floor. I screwed up my eyes, trying to see what was in the room with me – what I was sure had touched my face. All I could hear was the sound of my own hard, uneven breaths. But I could sense something coming closer, a shapeless darkness, pressing itself towards me as I lay on the bed, clutching my duvet, shivering and whimpering. I screwed my eyes shut, willing the thing to disappear, knowing it wouldn't. And then – something cold as earth – a finger, a nail – a sharp, violent clawing down my cheek. I screamed.

The door was flung open and yellow light from the landing swept in. Mum ran over to me and pulled me into a hug. I grabbed her and sobbed into her shoulder, gulping in her familiar safe smell of soap and toothpaste and tea.

She took me downstairs and made me hot milk, like she used to do when I was very little and wouldn't settle. She assured me there was no one in my room. 'I've even looked under your bed. You silly thing – you've scratched yourself on the face. It was just a very bad dream.' She even sat in the chair while I tried to sleep on the sofa, promising not to leave me on my own.

Even with Mum there, though and knowing I was safe from whatever nightmares might be in my room, I couldn't rest. Every time I almost fell asleep, pictures kept running through my brain. Zoe and I doing our ceremony this afternoon. The knife digging into the smooth flesh on our arms and the squeezed-out drops of blood. Kerry and creepy Dave and something about the way he looked at her. Zoe acting like someone I hardly knew.

17
Flat 1413

I couldn't believe it when Zoe knocked at the door at about nine the morning after Jodie's party, looking like nothing had ever happened. She waved her hands at me. 'Like the new perfume? It's disinfectant,' she said. 'I stink.'

I sniffed. 'Yeah, you do, a bit. How come?'

Zoe told me that she'd been to the empty flat and cleaned it up. 'I felt like a prat after last night,' she said. 'So I thought the least I could do was to go and mop up the mess. I bet it looks cleaner than it ever did in there.'

'It was never going to win a Beautiful Homes award,' I said. 'But yeah, the pile of vomit didn't really add to the atmos. I can't believe we left the key with you, the state you were in. I thought Kerry had it. How are you feeling?'

'Good.'

I had to admit she wasn't displaying any ill-effects. 'Shouldn't you have a stonking headache or something?'

'Apparently not.'

Zoe kept going on about what a laugh it had been and how she'd felt really amazing and liberated. It made me wonder if we'd actually been at the same party.

'Yeah, I went a bit far with the booze,' Zoe went on. 'But Anna, it was like – I don't know. It was like suddenly we could do whatever we wanted and no one could stop us.'

You, I thought. No one could stop you. There wasn't really an 'us', last night.

'We made that happen,' Zoe breathed. 'We asked for something to happen. And look what did.'

'It was just...' I didn't want to damp her down. But it hadn't felt so special to me. Except that, maybe, Kerry came into her own, didn't she? She went against all her rules, for us, but mainly for Zoe. There was a chance things would get better between them. 'Kerry was cool, wasn't she?'

Zoe ignored this. 'We got a gift, didn't we? Think about it. We got the keys to our own place.'

'Huh?'

'We've got somewhere to go, just the two of us. You're always moaning about the magic gear in your bedroom. We can store it there, can't we? And we can escape there, whenever we want to. It's the best thing.'

'I'll be glad to get rid of that stuff, that's for sure. It gives me nightmares.' Should I mention this to Zoe? Would she laugh at me? 'I keep thinking that... that someone's there, in my room.'

Zoe sat down on the stairs. 'Someone, like who?'

I shrugged, struggling to find a way to explain it. 'Maybe I mean something, not someone. But I feel all cold and –'

'Fix the heating.' Zoe smirked.

'No, it's a weird kind of cold. I think I can feel things touching me. Stop smiling at me like that. I mean it. I'm scared out of my head, every night.'

Zoe took my hand and squeezed it. 'Sorry. You're right – what we're doing is really powerful. I can feel things in your room too. But that's what's so exciting. It's not a bad presence or anything evil. It's just the spirits, getting us things we ask for. They're on our side.'

She pulled me up towards my room. 'Come on. I'm with you. Nothing's going to happen that you don't want.' I didn't even want to go in, but I followed Zoe and watched as she drew my curtains drawn and lit an incense stick.

"We need to get your dad back, for good,' Zoe announced. 'And I've got one or two people I want to take care of, just for me.'

This time Zoe had downloaded some meditation CD with strange, unearthly sounds on it and we stared and stared at the candle flame until my brain pounded and everything felt unreal. Even when I closed my eyes, I could see flickering and dancing, behind my eyelids, right inside in my head. Zoe started to chant, over and over again. And then she asked the spirits to banish anything bad from our lives. It was a warm morning, but I started to shiver. Painful little goose bumps rose all along my arms and the cold prickling down my neck and back felt as if tiny, sharp fingers were playing across my skin.

'Zoe,' I whispered.

"Shhh.'

I waited. But I could see them – black shapes moving in the dark recesses of the room. I felt tears pricking my eyes. 'Zoe, please.'

'What?' she hissed.

'I – I –' I bit my lip. 'I'm sorry. I'm really scared.'

Zoe looked at me, her eyes narrowed and a half-smile on her lips. 'You're kidding me, right?'

I shook my head. 'This is frightening me to death. I didn't think I believed in ghosts. Did you?'

Zoe looked around the room before she answered. 'Of course I do. I can feel them, right now. We asked for them and they came.' She smiled.

I took two or three deep breaths, to try to stop myself from crying in front of her. 'I want to stop all this. Please.'

'We can't stop now. It's too late. You can't wake up the spirits of the dead and then tell them, whoops, you're sorry, you didn't mean it.'

I looked into Zoe's eyes, but my vision blurred a little. She leaned forward and put her hands on my shoulders. 'Hey. Don't be upset. I promise they're good spirits. I know it. Look at all the stuff that's been happening.'

I wiped at my eyes.

'You want your dad back home for good, don't you?'

Before I got a chance to answer, there was a sudden piercing sound as someone pressed the doorbell hard. It went through our heads like a gunshot.

Zoe swore.

I stood up, blinking and a little dizzy.

'Don't answer it,' Zoe pleaded, but I couldn't do that.

'Clear up, will you?' I asked. 'And open the window. We can guess who it is.'

I was right. 'Hi,' I said, barely able to meet Kerry's eyes. 'You OK?'

It was typical. I was the only one who didn't drink a load of cider the night before, but somehow, I was the only one feeling nauseous. What was going on? Kerry lingered about on the doorstep and I knew I had to ask her inside. Zoe was going to go mad.

When I opened the bedroom door, all the ritual stuff had been tidied away. Zoe was getting very fast at that and the window was wide open, although the smell of the incense hung around. Sweet, though, not sulphurous. Zoe was sitting upright on my bed looking like Mary Poppins, all prim and innocent, flicking through a magazine.

'Oh,' she said to Kerry. 'It's you again.'

'Zoe,' I said. 'Kerry really helped you – us – out last night, remember.'

'Was that your shirt I had on?' Zoe asked.

Kerry nodded, grinning daftly and waiting to be thanked. 'I gave you one of my best ones.'

'Damn,' said Zoe. 'I used it to clean up the flat this morning. Then I put it in the bin.'

I could've slapped her.

'Tell me you're joking,' I said, when Kerry gave a nervous little laugh.

'Nope, sorry.' Zoe put her palm to her cheek and rolled her eyes. 'So stupid of me.'

I felt myself going red and hot and full of shame, although I'd had no part in this. I picked up the T-shirt Kerry had given me. 'Here,' I said, in a mumble. 'I washed it. Thanks, Kerry. I – I'm really sorry. You were great last night.'

Kerry took the top without a word. I didn't want to look at her face, so I kept staring at the ground.

There was a horrible silence. Then Kerry said, with forced cheerfulness, 'So, what shall we do today?'

'We?' Zoe was flicking through the magazine again, as if Kerry wasn't there.

'Want to go to the shops?' I suggested, sure that it was hopeless. 'I need a new bag for school. Mum left me some money.'

'No cash again,' said Zoe, without looking up. I knew she was going to be like this as long as Kerry was there.

'Well, I might – I might – just go home then.' Kerry had a catch in her voice. She wanted to be asked to stay and part of me wanted to make her feel better. But I could tell that Zoe would just freeze her out. Or torture her in some way.

'I guess,' I said.

I hated myself.

Kerry turned and I followed her down the stairs. 'Hey.' I caught her arm before she went out the door. 'I'm sorry. I don't know why Zoe is – I think she's just – I can't –'

Kerry shrugged.

I picked up the tenner Mum had left on the hall table and pushed it into Kerry's hand. 'Will this go towards a new top?'

She shoved it back at me, shaking her head, and I guessed she was going to cry again. I let her go. As I shut the door, I thought about her fearsome mum and knew that Kerry was going to get into huge trouble over the missing shirt.

'She gone?' Zoe came down the stairs. 'Good. Now we can go into town.'

'You said you didn't have any money,' I reminded her.

'That was just to get rid of her.'

'Did you have to be so –' Horrible, I wanted to say. Cruel.

'Cruel to be kind,' Zoe said, as if she'd plucked the word out of my head. 'I keep telling you, if we're nice to her, she'll haunt us for our whole lives. She was such an embarrassment last night. Having to look after her ruined the whole thing. She finally needs to get that we don't want her around – especially now we have our own place.'

We caught the bus into town and went to one of my favourite cafes, but I felt like I had maggots squirming around my insides and I couldn't even finish my burger. Zoe chatted all the time about all sorts of things – school, GCSEs, one of her latest arty projects. This was the Zoe I loved. A different Zoe to the one who could treat people so badly. I tried to push that Zoe out of my mind.

Just then, we heard loud sniggering and turned to see Maxine and some other girls from school, waiting to get a seat. 'Not sure we should stay here,' one of them was saying, loudly. 'It's the grimy goths, over in the corner. I thought there was a funny smell.'

Quite a few people turned to look at us. I stared at the remains of my coffee. Zoe muttered something under her breath.

'What did you say?' I asked them. Zoe had her eyes closed and was still muttering, too quietly for me to make out the words.

'We're saying there's a stink. Coming from you two.' The others held their noses and waved their hands.

Just then a woman strode over to them. 'I'll have to ask you to leave,' she said.

The gang burst out into protests. Zoe and I turned to stare.

'We haven't done anything,' Maxine said, while the others stood with their mouths open. 'You can't chuck us out.'

'It's quite obvious you're trying to cause trouble,' the woman said. 'I can hear you making rude remarks about other customers. You can see there are no free seats, anyway. Please leave.'

'I want to see the manager,' said Maxine.

'I am the manager,' said the woman.

Zoe and I grinned at each other.

As the girls turned to leave, one of them spat on the floor, in our general direction. 'That's it,' said the manager. 'You're all barred, permanently. Now get out.'

Then she came over to us. 'I'm very sorry,' she said. 'I heard what those girls were saying and I didn't like it at all. I've seen you in here a few times and you never cause trouble. I've seen them too and I swear they once left without paying. Choose a cake and another drink – on the house.'

We chose something from the menu and she went to get us a freebie. 'I can't believe that just happened,' I said to Zoe.

She gave me a slow smile. 'I willed something to happen to them,' she said. 'I just felt like I could do it. It was amazing, wasn't it?'

Afterwards, we went mooching round the shops. Zoe suddenly suggested buying Kerry a new top. 'I've only got a couple of quid, but if you lend me that money your mum gave you, I'll pay it back,' Zoe said, picking a T-shirt from the rack.

'Why?' I said. 'I mean, I think it is a good idea. But you said you wanted to get rid of Kerry.'

'Oh, I don't know. Call it karma,' said Zoe, peering at the size label. 'What do you think she is – size 12? Or 14? If we get a size too small, she'll be mortified and if I get one that's too big, it'll look like I'm making a comment about her size. I just feel a bit guilty, that's all. I don't want to be like that crowd from school.'

I squeezed her arm.

Guilt made us spend all our money on the top for Kerry and a bracelet in the same colour. The sort of shiny, pink-y thing she would wear. We knocked at her door with the new top in its bag. Her mum answered, shouted for Kerry and left us standing at the door. The way she looked at us made me shrink. It was like her mum-radar had picked up something rotten. Kerry sniffed when she saw us.

Zoe held out the top, which was wrapped in tissue paper. 'Got you this,' she said. 'To say sorry. I was a cow.'

Kerry's face lightened straight away and she tore at the tissue paper. She held it up against herself.

'Thanks,' she said and leaned forward as if she was going to give Zoe a hug. Zoe shrank back.

'Really, thanks,' Kerry said again. 'You were pretty horrible though.'

Zoe shrugged. 'One of those days. Can we forget it?'

Kerry nodded vigorously and as we turned to go, she followed us, closing her door behind her. 'So,' she said. 'What shall we do tonight?'

Zoe closed her eyes.

After we'd shaken Kerry off again, by an elaborate process of pretending we were each going home and then meeting up again near The Cut, Zoe persuaded me to go and look at her cleaning efforts in the empty flat. She still had the key and said she was planning to keep it, unless Jodie directly asked for it back.

Zoe gave a long sigh. 'We're back to Square One with Kerry,' she said. 'What was I thinking? Maybe she would have stayed away this time and then we'd be finished with her. Like cutting off an infected limb.'

'Don't let's go there again,' I said, blinking at the strong smell of bleach when we opened the door. When Zoe said she'd cleaned the place, she wasn't kidding. It smelled worse than a hospital. 'I felt awful. It was like shooting Bambi.'

'Yes, but,' said Zoe, rhythmically kicking at the wall with her toe, 'she gets on my nerves so much, Anna. I was sorry for her, for a few minutes, but now she thinks she's one of us, part of a little gang. I only want it to be just us two again.'

'So do I. But we've been through this again and again. She hasn't got anyone else. I think we're stuck.'

Zoe punched the wall then said, 'Owww' and examined her hand. I laughed at her and after a second or two she joined in.

'What about that café, though?' Zoe's eyes were firelight. 'Since we're talking about karma.'

We went over and over what had happened. Zoe insisted it was all down to our magic working.

'Or they brought it on themselves,' I said. 'Mouthing off like that.'

'Yes, but, when does anyone ever stop them? When do they ever get caught out like that? That Maxine strides round school like she owns the place and even the teachers think she's a saint. Magic, Anna. We've got the power.'

Zoe held out her hands. Her fingers were long and pale. Witch's fingers. I half expected to see bolts of lightning coming out of them. 'Tomorrow,' she said. 'We'll try again. Thinking about what we really, really want and ask for it. Imagine it happening. Imagine it coming true.'

'I guess. OK.' Zoe took my hand and I squeezed it. 'What will you ask for?'

Zoe shrugged. 'I've got some ideas. But it's almost a full moon. It's a good time to ask for things. To have more luck.'

We got a chance to try some more magic when my mum went out to do her weekly battle with the supermarket. Zoe took extra care in setting everything up. There were candles in the four corners of the room, or at least as close to the corners as we could get them without setting fire to something.

Zoe chanted out some more verses that she'd written herself. About summoning up all the powers of the sun and the moon, earth, air, fire and water – then asking for something I really wanted. It felt a bit like a being a kid about to blow out your birthday candles. You know it's a bit daft to make a wish, but you always do it anyway. So I asked.

Zoe just said something very vague about having more good luck. And then she said: 'And rid us of that Kerry. Please.' As we stared at the candle flames, which were absolutely still in the airless room, the wax was melting far too fast and spitting like a snake. I felt something brush past my shoulders and I jumped and gave a little shriek.

Zoe glared. 'What's the matter?'

I stared around the room. 'Something touched me.'

'Really?' Zoe looked at me eagerly.

I couldn't explain. 'Zoe.' I breathed in deeply because I knew she wouldn't want to hear this. 'You know I keep having these awful dreams. Do you think if we stopped doing these rituals, they might go away?'

Zoe considered. 'No, I think the dreams are just your imagination running off with you. Look, when I summon up the dead, the main person I have in mind is my dad. I think if anyone's spirit was going to help me, it would be his. So yes, I think there are presences in the room, but I don't think there's anything evil floating around, if that's what you're worrying about.'

My shoulders drooped. 'I know. But the nightmares won't stop. I don't even like being here during the day on my own. Don't laugh at me!'

'I'm not. But I really think you're just getting worked up about nothing.' She knelt back on her heels. 'This is why no one tries ... magic, or whatever you want to call it. Things start to happen and they get so spooked they give up. But we're doing it.' She breathed out, her eyes glittering. 'It feels like our powers get stronger every day. Let's see what happens, eh?'

On the walk home, I got a call from Luke. He told me that he'd agreed to go with Kerry to stay with some cousins for a couple of weeks, almost until the end of the holidays.

'I'm sorry,' he said. 'But Mum's had enough of us hanging around the house all summer. She just suddenly snapped, I don't know why. We thought Kerry might be a bit much for my aunt to handle on her own, so I said I'd go too.'

'I'll miss you,' I said.

'I'll miss you too.' We lingered on the phone for a few more minutes, not saying much.

When Luke hung up, I felt even more down. Zoe had her wish and we were rid of Kerry, but that meant I'd lost Luke too, for a while. Not that Zoe would care about that.

When I got home and put my key in the door, I could hear Mum and Dad laughing. Dad was back, then. I peered into the living room. They were fussing over a huge golden Labrador dog that turned and gave a deep bark when he saw me.

'What's going on?'

'This is Barney,' said Dad. 'I'm supposed to be looking after him for a friend.'

'What – here?' I gave Mum a questioning look. She wasn't mad on dogs. And we definitely couldn't afford one.

'Just for a little while,' Dad said.

Barney padded up to me, his tail wagging rhythmically. He nuzzled my leg and I felt his warm, moist breath on my fingers as I reached down to stroke him. 'Hey, Barney,' I said. I swear he smiled.

I caught Mum and Dad sharing a glance. 'We thought – maybe you could keep him in your room at nights,' Mum said.

'He's used to kipping on his owner's bed,' Dad said. 'And it might make you feel a bit safer.'

I knelt down to get to know Barney a bit better. 'Thanks,' I said. 'He's gorgeous. I'll give it a try.'

We took Barney out for a walk. I had the dog on his lead, pulling me along and my other arm linked in Dad's. I couldn't remember the last time I'd felt so safe. 'This was a brilliant idea,' I said, laughing as Barney tugged me forward and we had to half-run to keep up. 'Doesn't his owner mind?'

'It's not for long, so don't fall in love with the daft mutt. But it might get you past these horrible nightmares you're having.'

When I wanted to go to bed, I took my mug of hot chocolate and clicked my fingers for Barney to come with me up the stairs. He leaped up and followed. But after a few steps, he stopped and pricked up his ears, staring straight ahead.

'Come on, boy,' I urged him. 'Bed time.'

I got him to follow me as far as the landing. Outside my bedroom door, his body went rigid and he began a low, steady growl.

I swallowed. 'What is it, Barney?' I pushed at the door and felt the familiar cold air waiting for me. The dog's growl grew louder. His whole body was vibrating. I took a shivering step into the room. Barney turned and threw himself towards the stairs, letting out a howl that seemed to shake the whole house.

Mum and Dad flew out of the living room, jumping back as Barney darted between them. 'What the –' Mum ran out of words.

'He won't go in the room,' I said, gulping back my urge to cry. 'He knows there's something in there.'

'But there isn't,' Mum sighed. 'We've checked and checked. You know that.'

Dad rubbed Barney's head. 'He's usually the most placid dog ever. I don't know what would make him act like that.' He beckoned me down the stairs. 'Come on, looks like it's you on the sofa tonight. With Barney. I'll stay in your room. OK?'

The next day, Zoe texted to say she'd won an art competition in the local paper. The prize was vouchers for the expensive art supplies shop in town. She was really pleased with herself. *Cm & help me spend*, she messaged me. When I replied and told her that Kerry was going away for a while, she sent me back a row of exclamation marks.

'You know why it happened,' Zoe said, seriously, as we sat over two creamy lattes. 'It happened because of the magic. Same as the other day. I asked for good luck. That's why I won this and that's why we've got rid of Kerry for a few days.'

'No, you won that 'cause you're really good at art,' I said.

Zoe looked down at her mug and swirled the spoon around. 'Not that good,' she shrugged. 'You should see what my mum can do. She should've been a proper artist.'

I hadn't heard this before. 'What happened?'

Zoe shrugged. 'She had me.'

'And?'

Zoe licked froth from her spoon, delicate as a kitten. 'She had to give college up. She never really got the chance to go back. I think that's why she –'

I waited. 'Why she what?'

Zoe glanced away. 'Why she's so proud of me, of course.' Her tone was sarcastic.

'Right.' Why she's always angry with you, you mean. That thought came out of nowhere but now that I had it, it all seemed very clear. 'You never told me that before, about your mum.'

'Why would I?'

'Because,' I thought about it for a minute. 'Because maybe that's why your mum is always so horrible. You say she's always having a go at you. But maybe she's kind of jealous. Because she's bored and frustrated.'

Zoe curled her lip. 'I'm the one who's bored and frustrated. She never tries to understand me. I don't see why I should try for her.'

Zoe looked around. I could tell she was looking for a way to change the subject. She hated talking about her mum and I guessed she wished she hadn't mentioned her. Suddenly her face brightened. 'I've had a great idea,' she said.

'Why does that make me nervous?'

Zoe laughed. 'No, listen. That empty flat.'

'What about it?'

'We can go there whenever we want. Let's move all that ritual stuff there too, and then you can stop going on about it being in your bedroom.'

'Now that part of it does sound like a great idea,' I said. The thought of clearing my room of that sinister skull and everything else – and of holding our ceremonies somewhere where I didn't have to sleep – sounded just what I needed.

'One thing,' Zoe said.

I raised my eyebrows at her in a question.

'Kerry has absolutely not got to hear about this. If she gets involved it'll spoil everything. This flat is just for us two. Promise me, Anna.'

I promised her, of course. This was Zoe. I'd still have promised her just about anything.

18

Three's a crowd

Ever since the night Barney arrived I'd slept downstairs on the sofa, the dog heavy and comforting across my legs. Dad had taken my room, but he was convinced that Barney could smell something that we couldn't.

'There might be a dead rat under the floorboards or something,' he said, making Mum shudder. 'Something that's decomposed and we can't smell it, but a dog can. I don't know. But we ought to get to the bottom of it, so Anna can have her room back. Maybe I should completely gut it and redecorate?'

That made Zoe and I pack up the ritual gear from my room and take it all to the flat as soon as we could, before someone found it. But nothing would make Barney go in there, all the same. In spite of what Dad said, I already loved that dog – the way he was so pleased to see me, his tail wagging like a windscreen wiper, the way he was always ready for a warm hug.

One morning – after I'd spent the previous day with my mum – I had a text. *Meet at flat asap. Surprise 4 u.*

She wasn't kidding. I swallowed down my horror of being in the lift alone to go to the top storey and I tapped on the door of 1413. Zoe opened it. I was hit by the smell of paint. 'Welcome,' she said, with a huge grin. Beyond the door was a narrow corridor, with doors to each room. Zoe had covered the walls with posters of bands and pages from arty magazines and old concert flyers.

I walked in to the main living room and looked around, open-mouthed. Zoe had painted the walls in a kind of a purple colour. It was a dark shade, but it was a big room, with huge undressed windows, so it still felt light. She'd put an old rug and some cushions on the floor and more posters on the walls.

'Where'd you get these from?' I asked, flopping down on one of the cushions.

'Box room at home.' Zoe looked around, with a satisfied expression.

'Wow. These cushions look new.'

'We don't use it very often. I only bought the paint. What do you think, then? I spent all day yesterday doing it – and half the night too.'

'I bet you did. It's really good,' I said. 'But why?'

'I told you – this really is our place now,' Zoe said. 'The idiots who left didn't get the water turned off and Jodie's Dave did something with a bit of copper wire and got the power back on. There was a grungy old mattress in one room and some cups and plates, so I reckon the last tenants did a flit for some reason and didn't tell the council. We could bring a kettle and a heater and stuff, if we could get them from somewhere. We could even stay the night if we wanted.'

'I know,' I said. 'But Zoe, Jodie said the flats are going to be knocked down soon.'

'Yeah.' Zoe waved her hands at me. 'But it can't be, like, next week or anything, because there are still people living here. I'm sure the council has to find them new places to live before they can bring the bulldozers in.'

'I suppose.' I looked around and tried not to stare at the window. 'Wish it wasn't so high up.'

Zoe laughed at me and pressed herself against the glass, arms wide like an angel. 'I love it.'

'Stop it,' I said, squeezing my eyes shut. 'I can't even watch.'

We began to spend all our spare time at the empty flat. Zoe named it Whit's End and almost every time I went, something new was there. I soon found out how she was furnishing the place.

One afternoon, after we'd been to town, Zoe persuaded me to get off the bus a stop too early because she wanted to go to one of the big supermarkets on a nearby trading estate. She wouldn't tell me exactly what she was going to buy. She insisted that I didn't come in with her, but waited right at the entrance to the car park. When I asked why, she shook her head. 'You'll see in a minute,' was all she would say.

I lingered for around quarter of an hour, tapping impatiently at my phone. Then I spotted Zoe trundling towards me, a wire trolley in front of her, loaded with boxes. 'What have you –' I started, but Zoe kept walking and staring fixedly ahead.

'Just keep going,' she said, out of the side of her mouth. I followed her, striding fast to keep up, out of the trading estate and down a long street. After a few minutes, she glanced behind her and gave a long breath out. She manoeuvred the trolley into the drive of a boarded-up house.

'What the hell is all this stuff?' I asked.

Zoe gave me a huge smile. 'I've just got us a kettle, a microwave and a duvet,' she said.

I opened my mouth for a few minutes. 'How did you afford all that?'

Zoe gave me one of her 'you-are-so-stupid' looks. 'I didn't pay for them, that's how.'

'But –'

'Don't say anything. I really don't need a lecture. It's not like the supermarkets will miss the odd thing. They expect the odd bit of shoplifting.'

'They expect you to slide a bar of chocolate down your trousers, maybe, not walk out with a microwave,' I said. 'How did you manage it?'

'Actually, it's much easier than nicking bars of chocolate,' Zoe said. 'The security guys are on the lookout for people fiddling with their coats and pockets and stuff. Although–' she opened her long coat and handed me a packet of biscuits. 'I'm quite good at that too.'

As we wheeled the trolley in the direction of the flats, Zoe said she'd watched someone steal things from the supermarket before. If there was a tag, you could get rid of it with nail clippers, usually, she told me. 'You have to make sure the security guy is somewhere else, for a start. Then you just need to hold your nerve and walk past the self-service tills like you've already paid for it all. I've seen it done. I knew I could do it too.'

'Won't you be on a CCTV or something?'

'Yes, but they only go through the CCTV if they're looking for evidence. If they don't realise there's been a theft, they won't go back through it.'

'I'm not sure that's right,' I said. 'And they might be watching out for you if you go back there.'

Zoe shrugged. 'I won't, then. At least not for a while. There are loads of other supermarkets to pick.'

It was just our luck, though, that the lift wasn't working that day. We were dragging the boxes slowly and awkwardly up the concrete stairs when we met Dave on his way home. It was the only time I'd ever been pleased to see him, especially when he took the heavy microwave box and carried it for us.

'Jodie said you'd more or less moved in,' he said, winking at us.

Zoe gave him a quick smile, but curled her lip behind his back.

'I wouldn't call it moving in,' I said, trying not to look at the dark drop in between the flights of steps. 'We just use it now and then. To listen to music and stuff. We don't live there.'

'You stay there sometimes, though,' Dave said, nodding at Zoe. 'All night.' He stopped as we reached the top floor and Zoe dug in a pocket for the key. 'So you're on your own then?'

Zoe shook her head. 'I only stay if my boyfriend's with me.'

'Your invisible boyfriend, yeah.' Dave carried the box into the kitchen and put it down on the bench. He rolled up his sleeves. His arms were taut, inked over with tattoos. 'Not going to offer me a drink to say thanks?'

'We haven't got anything. Sorry,' Zoe said.

Dave leaned an elbow on the bench and smiled at us. 'How are you going to thank me, then, ladies?'

That sick, hot feeling rushed through me again. I stared at the floor.

Zoe marched back to the door and held it open. 'By not telling your girlfriend you've been flirting with us?'

Dave let out a short laugh. 'Another time, then, eh?' And he left.

We looked at each other and Zoe pretended to stick her fingers in her mouth and gag.

'He's been watching you,' I said. 'Don't stay here on your own, Zoe. It mightn't be safe. He knows there isn't really a boyfriend.'

Zoe made a *pfff*ing noise with her lips. 'I love staying here. I'm not going to let that creep stop me.'

'Don't you get scared on your own?'

'Scared? Never. When I can't sleep I just stand and look out of the window. It makes me feel like I'm on top of a mountain or something. Like if I jumped out I could just spread my arms and I'd fly. Float. Like a silver seagull.'

I shivered.

Despite all this, it was brilliant having somewhere of our own to go to. There was a niggly, anxious part of me that half-expected the police to knock on the door and tell us we were squatting there illegally, or that we were being arrested for having a flat full of stolen goods. Things just appeared: bedding, a music dock, even a toaster. I kept telling Zoe to stop it and that she was going to get caught, but when I did she just laughed. And in the tiny kitchen there was always soup, tea, chocolate, bread. Everything found its way to the flat via Zoe's coat pockets or else she coolly walked out of a shop holding a big box in front of her, with the confidence of someone who'd paid. She used a different supermarket every time, she told me – and she always watched it for a little while first to see what she could get away with. Whenever we had something to eat or drink, Zoe would make a joke about disposing of the evidence. She insisted the spirits were taking care of her. 'I kind of imagine that I'm invisible,' she said, laughing. 'It seems to work.'

The only place she didn't steal from was Dead Bouquet. She said it was too small and didn't make enough profit, so it would be immoral.

The best thing that happened, as we slid towards the end of the damp summer holidays and into a grey September, was Luke coming back home. It meant Kerry came back too, of course, so it was one of those situations where my mum would joke that 'every silver lining has a cloud'. I met up with Luke at the bus stop the day before term started again. I'd been worried that I might feel awkward about him, after a two-week break, so I took Barney with me for moral support, but when Luke saw me he held his arms wide open and I just ran into him and into a tight, tight hug.

'I've really missed you, Anna.' He kissed the top of my head. I loved it when he did that. His body was always warm. I'd missed his clean, shower-gel smell and the way he'd wrap his jacket round me to keep me warm too.

I asked him how Kerry had enjoyed her break. He laughed. 'Yes, she loved it. You know how she goes into everything like it's all so exciting, like a great big kid.' He paused to stroke Barney's ears. 'She talked about you all the time, though. It's like a badge of honour for her, having you as a friend. My aunt said at one point that if she heard any more about the Amazing Anna she would scream.'

Luke's course and his part-time job meant we were not going to be able to see each other as much as we wanted, but we started texting each other dozens of times a day and calling every night. Given that I was supposed to start thinking about exams, it wasn't the right time to break it to Mum or Dad that I had a boyfriend anyway – in my head, I could already hear their list of objections. Anyway, seeing less of Luke would keep Zoe off my back.

Even once we were back at school, Zoe and I spent as much time as possible at Flat 1413. We worked out a system for getting rid of Kerry every day at the edge of The Cut. We would make like we were going home but after a few minutes we'd sneak back and meet up again, right in the middle of The Cut, and go to the flats. My mum thought we were spending more time with our made-up mate, Emma Wood, because I told her the imaginary Emma had a better sound system.

Almost every time I went, I noticed more of Zoe's stuff in the bathroom and little piles of her clothes on the floor. I asked if her mum didn't mind her staying out all night. 'I tell her I'm at yours, if she ever asks,' Zoe said.

'I wish you wouldn't,' I said. 'What if she comes looking for you?'

'She won't,' Zoe said. 'She's just glad to get rid of me most of the time.'

As for me: I couldn't work out what was going on with my mum and dad. He was still with us, but he kept saying how he should find his own place and stop taking advantage of Mum. He looked sad all the time. A little older, the frown line between his brows getting deeper. And Mum was snappier than usual.

I kept hoping to walk in and find them holding hands or something, announcing with silly grins that the divorce was all one big mistake and that they were getting back together again for good. But it didn't happen.

One morning, when Mum found herself tripping over the lead to Dad's laptop, she actually swore. Mum almost never swore.

'Excuse me,' I said, half-laughing. 'If I used that kind of language you'd go mad.'

'I'm sorry.' Mum winced. 'But it's getting beyond a joke, isn't it? This place just isn't big enough for three. The extra cash is nice, of course, but…' She sighed and ran her hand through her hair. 'And that dog… I know you're fond of him, but he's so big and drippy.'

'It's good to have Dad around again, though, isn't it?' I asked. 'He fixed that blocked drain the other day and you said it saved you calling a plumber.'

'Yes, all of that's great.' Mum stopped and sighed. I could see her choosing her words. 'And it must be nice for you to have him around, I know. It's just... all gone on a bit longer than I expected.'

Yeah, for me too, I thought. But not in the way that you mean.

One late Saturday afternoon in October, when it was already dark, we only had candlelight and the air in the flat's main room was thick with the scent of incense. We played Ghost Dance at a low-ish volume. It felt like the presence in the room was so close I felt I could reach out and touch it, so solid I half expected it to speak to me.

Zoe ended every ritual with the words: 'And please. Get rid of her.' At first, I'd always assumed she was talking about Kerry. But I started to wonder. Zoe would rather spend cold, damp nights on a mattress in the empty flat than go home. And although we both had cuts on our hands and arms from the blood part of the rituals, I'd noticed, when we got changed for games at school, that Zoe's bruises had all but gone.

I sat staring into the candle flames. Zoe blinked and gazed out of the big bare window at the black sky with its odd, sparse star. And there was a loud thumping at the door.

My heart quickened. I was about to get up, but Zoe shook her head at me. 'No one knows we're here,' she whispered. 'We shouldn't answer it. They'll have to go away.'

But the knocking went on. Then a voice shouted through the letterbox. 'It's only me, Jodie,' she said. 'Answer the door, you two. I know you're in there.'

Zoe sighed and hauled herself up, while I made a grab for the skull and the bowl of earth and shoved them behind a cushion. And when Zoe opened the door, Jodie was there. With Kerry. They walked in without being asked.

'Kerry didn't know you used this place,' Jodie said. 'And then she was too shy to come up and see you on her own, I don't know why. I said you wouldn't mind.'

I tried to smile at Kerry, who stared around the room, taking in the posters on the walls, Zoe's drawings, the mugs we'd left lying around.

Jodie laughed. 'They've made themselves quite at home, haven't they?'

Kerry said, 'Yes,' in a quiet sort of a voice.

'You know,' Jodie went on, 'I don't mind you being here. Better than the place being empty, I think. But I should warn you – someone came around to read the meters the other day. They were knocking at all the doors. It's only a matter of time before someone switches your power off again. And your water. So don't get too comfortable, you lot.'

She went to get ready for a night out. And we were left with Kerry. Zoe hadn't said a word since she'd arrived.

'Kerry,' I said, jumping up, 'Want a drink?'

'What kind of a drink?' Kerry looked around, as if she expected someone or something to jump out at her.

'Absinthe,' said Zoe, folding her arms and glaring at Kerry. 'Mixed with puppy's blood.'

I tried to laugh. 'Take no notice,' I said. 'Hot chocolate, as usual. Or mint tea.' I hurried into the little kitchen then popped my head back round the doorway. 'Biscuit?'

Kerry followed me. 'How long have you been coming here?'

'Oh,' I said, busying myself with the shiny kettle and keeping my face turned away from Kerry, because I always think people can tell when I'm fibbing. 'Not long. Week or two, or something like that.'

Kerry's expression was sulky. 'Jodie says you've been coming here since the summer.'

I took a breath. 'I don't think it's that long,' I said, as vaguely as possible. I could sense Zoe's fury, as if it was rolling at me in waves.

'But you never said.' Kerry looked down her nose at the mug I'd just slid along the kitchen bench. 'You never asked me to come along.' She paused for a minute as if she was daring herself to ask. 'Why not?'

'We —' I tried waving a packet of chocolate biscuits at Kerry, but she shook her head. 'We thought we'd get it all nice first.'

I heard Zoe make a small, explosive, spluttering sound.

Kerry looked watery-eyed. 'It feels like you were just keeping me out of things,' she said. 'Again.'

'Yes, well,' Zoe started, but I interrupted. 'No, it's just you were away at the end of the summer, weren't you? And then we thought, let's get it looking really good and give you a bit of a surprise.'

Kerry looked as if she wanted to believe me, but Zoe ruined it by shaking her head.

'Does Luke know about this place?' Kerry asked.

I swallowed. 'No.'

'Why not?'

I couldn't find a reply. The real answer was: because he would have told you. And we didn't want you to know.

'I wanted it kept a secret,' Zoe said, suddenly. 'We're not really supposed to be here, right? I said that the fewer people know, the better.'

'Oh.' Kerry nodded. She flicked on the light switch in the main room, and looked around it. In the full glare of the bare electric lightbulb, you could see where Zoe's paint had smeared a little across the floor and the dusty skirting boards. You could see where a damp patch had made its way back through the fresh paint, in a dark grey bloom. You could see how sad the place really was. Kerry was silent for a few beats. Then she said: 'I like your drawings, Zoe.'

Zoe nodded. But she looked like she wanted to strangle Kerry. I knew that now, our special place wouldn't be the same.

19

Caught

The day before my birthday Dad said he would take me into town and buy me something, if I could decide what it was I wanted. But I couldn't – all I really wanted was some cash so that we could get more stuff for the flat and so Zoe would stop walking out of shops with things she hadn't paid for. And also, so that we could get some clothes from Dead Bouquet. I could hardly tell Dad about the flat and he wasn't keen on buying me anything to wear. He steered me towards the computer shop and started talking me through the specs on all the shiny laptops. He even stroked one of them. 'Buy yourself one,' I suggested, after he'd droned on with some nerdy sales guy for about twenty minutes.

But in the end, to shut him up, I chose some sleek black thing and it all got boxed up with a load of extra bits and pieces that I didn't understand or care about. Dad locked it into the boot of his car and took me out for lunch.

We talked for a bit about school and exams and all that stuff that parents find so endlessly fascinating. And then he said: 'Look. We're still a bit worried about you, Anna. You're never in the house these days. We don't know anything about this new friend of yours, this Emma. And your sleeping problem's not getting any better. You look so pale and tired. Your mum says every time she mentions it, you change the subject.'

'Cold weather today, isn't it,' I said and gave a little giggle. Dad didn't laugh with me.

'Why are you so determined not to go to the doctors?'

I shifted in my chair. 'Because it's just – it's just exams and stuff. It'll get better when they're all done.'

'You would tell us – me or your mum – if there was something else? You know we only want to help?'

I sighed hard. 'Yeah, yeah, I would. It's nothing. And anyway, all a doctor would do is bang on about teenage hormones and periods and stuff.'

That worked. Dad's gaze shifted sideways and I could see him grasping around in his head for something else to talk about.

I helped him out. 'Anyway, what about you?'

'Me? What about me?'

I topped up the fizzy water in my glass. 'Are you going to get back together with Mum?'

Dad looked as if I'd thrown my water at him. 'Whatever made you – Is that what you thought was happening?'

I stared back at him. 'Well, you've been living with us for weeks now. I thought, maybe –' Suddenly I was wishing I hadn't asked.

Dad rubbed his eyes. He looked really worn out. 'I'm sorry. I shouldn't have moved in with you and your mum at all. I should've just found my own place. I've given you completely the wrong idea.'

'You have?'

'Anna, sweetheart. I know you don't like me talking about Ellie, but – fact is – I loved her. I still do. And I miss her. I haven't found my own place because I keep hoping she'll have me back.'

I swallowed. 'Right.' My eyes started to sting a little and I screwed them up. 'So you just used Mum. All you wanted was somewhere to kip.'

I might've raised my voice, because Dad glanced around to see if anyone was looking at us. 'It wasn't like that at all, and your mum knows it, even if you didn't. When we split up, we both agreed it was the best thing. Your mum wouldn't want me back, even if I asked her.'

'That's not true.' I had to wipe my eyes and I inspected my fingers for smears of mascara. 'Mum was heartbroken about the divorce. She was in bits, for ages.'

Dad nodded. 'We were both in bits. For ages. But that didn't make it the wrong thing to do.'

A waitress put plates down in front of us. We both stared at them for a few minutes. Neither of us started to eat.

'The other thing is, Anna – I'm sorry – but Barney's going to have to go back home.'

'No!' My shoulders slumped. 'But he's so happy with us. I love him. Can't you ask your friend if he'd let us keep him?'

'I can't, no.' Dad looked down at the table. 'She's back from her holiday and I was always only looking after him while she was away.'

'She?' It suddenly hit me. 'That's Ellie's dog, isn't it?'

Dad nodded. 'I'm sorry. I only ever meant him to cheer you up, to keep you company at nights. But he has to go back now. Ellie's missed him too.'

'Like I care what that spoiled princess thinks,' I muttered. My insides felt heavy. It wasn't fair: I loved Barney. He

197

loved me. Ellie seemed to get everything she wanted. Everything I wanted.

Back at home, Mum asked how the shopping trip had gone. I told her I'd got a new laptop.

'Aren't you lucky?' she said, but her smile looked a bit frosty and she gave Dad a sharp look. Dad set it all up for me and later, as I sat tapping at the keyboard and listening to music, I could hear them shouting at each other in the kitchen. How had I ever thought they were getting it together again? I felt like a stupid kid, one who'd told myself a great big fairytale.

Dad wasn't around the next morning when I came downstairs. Mum was there, cooking bacon and eggy bread. In fact, the smell woke me up, though I wasn't hungry. 'Special breakfast,' she said, over-brightly. She gave me a hard hug. 'Happy birthday, love.'

There were cards – one from Mum and a separate one from Dad. They used to sign the same one. And a card from my gran with a £20 note in it. Mum had got me a few books and a voucher to download some music. There were strawberry-scented soaps and some shower gel in a box and a pair of silver earrings. 'I love them,' I told Mum. 'Thanks.'

'Not as good as a laptop,' she said, laughing, but with a little edge in her voice.

'That was for Dad, not me. You know what he's like,' I said. Mum laughed again, properly this time. Later, over coffee, I got up the nerve to ask Mum if she wanted to get back together with Dad. If she said the same as Dad did yesterday, then I'd have to rethink.

'That's hardly likely, Anna,' she said.

'No, I know. But – if it was?'

Mum shook her head. 'You know, we weren't happy together. Not for a long time. Getting divorced is so awful that, when it first happened, I thought I'd never get through it. But it was only when he came back the other week that I remembered something. When he moved out to be with Ellie, I was hurt, yes. But more than anything else, I was relieved.'

'Relieved?'

Mum gave a little sigh. 'No more rows. No more having to walk out of the room to stop myself screaming at him.' There was a trace of a smile on her lips. 'Being my own boss, if you like.'

'Oh.' I'd misread things. Massively. I felt so dumb. 'So even if... so you don't want...'

Mum reached across the table and squeezed my hand. 'I'm sorry. That's not what you wanted to hear, is it? But I've moved on. Just like your dad. We're OK with what's happened. We just need you to be fine with it too.'

I bit my lip.

Zoe came with a card she'd made herself and a moonstone ring from Dead Bouquet, one I'd tried on a couple of weeks ago. I wore it as we sat at the kitchen table and Zoe painted my nails a midnight blue.

'I was thinking,' she murmured, making sure Mum wasn't in earshot, 'We could have a Halloween party at the flat. Wouldn't that be amazing? It could be a late birthday party for you too.'

I nodded. 'Who would we ask?'

'Some people from the shop and maybe Jodie too. She asked us to her party. She could bring a few mates too. There'd be a good crowd.' She paused. 'You could ask Luke if you want.'

I smiled at her. I knew she wasn't mad on Luke and she'd been moody yesterday when I'd told her he was taking me out tonight. Plus, asking Luke would mean asking Kerry. We couldn't really get out of that, I knew.

'Might not be his sort of thing. I'll think about it.'

Zoe started to paint tiny silver stars on my nails. 'I'll get loads of stuff for decorations,' she said. 'Or I could paint stuff on the walls. That'd be good.'

'Don't spend lots of money,' I said. What I meant was, don't go pinching stuff just for this.

Luke was kind of quiet when I went to meet him. It's the sort of thing I pick up straight away – someone else's mood. Only no one is ever honest about it, or at least not at first. They will keep saying everything is fine and no, nothing's wrong, until you're driven mad with the thing you know they're not saying. And after a hundred asks, they might eventually tell you what's the matter.

Luke was just the same. He had a cloud around him. I wondered if he was fed up because Zoe kept texting me, though I hadn't replied. I didn't even read the messages. Eventually, I even put my phone off and that still didn't lift the atmosphere. I started thinking that secretly he wanted to break up with me, but just wasn't saying so because it was my birthday. In the end, I asked him outright if that was what it was.

His mouth opened for a moment before he replied. 'No, it's not that, Anna, I – I think about you all the time. I'd hate it if we split up.'

'You have to tell me what's wrong then,' I said.

Luke snapped a bread stick into three parts and curled the paper up into a tight spiral shape. 'Kerry's been telling me about this empty flat.'

'Oh,' I said. Not telling Luke about it suddenly seemed really sneaky.

'Is Zoe actually living there?' Luke asked.

'No, 'course not, don't be daft.' I hesitated. 'She's spent a couple of nights there, though.'

Luke raised his eyebrows.

'I haven't,' I added, quickly.

'Kerry thinks there is all sorts of stuff in there – new things – and that Zoe's more or less moved in.'

I shook my head. 'That's not true.'

Luke played around with the rolled-up paper for another minute or two. 'Anna. I need to know. Why are you so mad on that Zoe? I don't get it.'

I hadn't expected this. 'She's my best friend. You know that. I really like her.'

'But why? I could understand it when you first moved to the school and you got stuck with her. But now you know how mean she is to my sister, most of the time. And she's so – well. Everyone thinks she's a loony-tune.'

I pouted. 'I don't.'

'She does crazy stuff,' Luke said. 'Kerry says she steals. I'm worried she's going to drag you into it too.'

'Well, that's not going to happen.' I pushed my plate away. How come every time someone treated me these days, I ended up having some sort of a row and getting put off my food? 'But don't expect me to abandon Zoe. I know she and Kerry don't get on. Don't ask me to take sides.'

'I'm not.' Luke pushed his plate away too. 'OK, maybe I am. Zoe isn't a very nice person. You are. And it's not like Kerry and Zoe are as bad as each other. Kerry can't stand up to someone like her.'

I shrugged. 'I like Zoe. I – I love Zoe. I won't drop her. It's up to Kerry if she wants to hang around me. But Zoe will always be there.'

Luke made a defeated sort of a face.

But the next day, when I tried to call Zoe, she wasn't answering. Maybe, I thought, she was angry because I'd ignored a string of messages from her last night, asking me to call when I was out with Luke. It wasn't till early evening when she finally texted back. *At flat. Cm round asap pls x.*

When she opened the door, she looked even paler than usual. She didn't speak, just held the door open and followed me back inside. Already, the place was covered in fake cobwebs and she'd painted a mural like a cemetery on the walls of the narrow entrance hall. I told her I thought it was brilliant. I had to say that, though if I was being honest, the place had started to give me the creeps, even without all the decorations. I tried to convince myself I was imagining things – after all, if I still had some kind of spirits in my bedroom, then why would they be here too? Or maybe they didn't exist at all, as I told myself every morning, without much effect.

Zoe flopped onto the cushions on the floor. 'Anna, something happened yesterday.'

She looked like someone had pricked her with a pin and let all her life out. 'What's up?'

Zoe started plaiting the ends of her long hair. 'I got caught trying to nick something.'

My insides felt suddenly curdled. 'Oh, god. You didn't. Where? What happened?'

'It was in the mall. It was just some stupid make-up. I didn't even really need it. I thought I'd got away with it, because I'd walked quite a way from the shop and suddenly this horrible woman in a uniform got hold of my arm. They made me tip out my bag and pockets, in front of all these people who just stopped and watched. It was awful.'

I shuffled over to her and put my arms around her. 'Poor you. Then what happened?'

'They made me tell them where I lived and then they took me home. In a police car.'

I swore, in a whisper.

'They told my mother what I'd done. That was awful. And then they gave me a caution because they said it was my first offence. But I'm banned from the shop.'

I gave her a hard hug. 'I'm sorry. What did your mum say?'

Zoe leaned her head on my shoulder. 'What do you think? She was furious, of course. She went up like a rocket as soon as the police had gone.' Zoe almost never cried.

But I could see her eyes were shining and wet and she blinked hard and sniffed.

I didn't know what to say to make her feel better. We sat in silence for a while. It was dark outside and there were only her candles for light. Shadows loomed around Zoe like black, ragged birds. 'I'm staying here tonight,' Zoe said. 'Any chance you could stay too?'

I thought about it. 'It'd be tricky. My mum would ask a lot of awkward questions. Wouldn't yours? 'Specially now?'

Zoe just sighed. 'I'm trying to keep right out of her way.'

She stood up and started putting out all the equipment for another ritual. 'I'm so glad I've got this place,' she said, as I watched, not helping. Candles in position. Incense. Blood-smeared skull. Knife. Bowl of graveyard dirt. 'It's somewhere to hide. Somewhere for me. And you, of course.'

'You need to watch out, though,' I said. 'Kerry's not happy. She's told Luke about this place. If we keep pushing her away, I reckon she'll cause trouble for us.'

Zoe made a face. 'I really don't care about Kerry. Let her do her worst.'

Zoe pulled out the rolled-up piece of paper where she'd written the words for our rituals and started to chant. I joined in to make her feel better. She rolled up her sleeve and I could see how many fresh scars and scabs there were. I wondered how often Zoe used the knife on herself and whether it was always part of a ritual. This time, before she pushed the knife back into her arm, I moved a candle closer so the soft yellow light played over her skin. There weren't just cuts. Red marks too, that would turn into deep bruises. I took hold of her wrist and ran my hand up her arm. And I looked her in the eye. 'Your mum?'

Her lip trembled. There were black shapes all around her, circling her like birds of prey.

I swallowed. 'Tell someone,' I said.

Zoe shook her head. Her eyes spilled into huge tears and she started to sob.

20

Halloween

It was October 31st. All Zoe talked about for days was the party. Every spare inch of wall in the flat was painted in black or purple, with designs of graves and vampires and skeletons. Some of the kids who hung around Dead Bouquet promised they were coming. Zoe had put the address on the little notice board in the shop and wrote: 'All goths welcome.' Jodie said she would come along with some mates before they went on to the pub and maybe afterwards too. I'd asked Luke in the end, but he was working that night. Kerry said she wasn't coming either, because her church told them it was wrong to celebrate pagan festivals like Halloween. I asked her a couple of times, just to make it sound as if I'd truly like her to come, but she wouldn't change her mind.

'Good,' Zoe said. 'Suit yourself.'

I persuaded Zoe not to go on any more shopping trips on her own. I couldn't be sure she wouldn't end up in the back of another cop car. So we went to a supermarket together – making sure it was one that would definitely not have CCTV photos of Zoe up on their walls. We used my birthday money and bought a load of party food and soft drinks, because neither of us could get away with looking eighteen. Jodie promised to get some booze and we told the Dead Bouquet people to bring some if they could. 'Otherwise we might as well have cake and jelly,' Zoe said. 'We don't want to look like little cutesy kiddies.'

We made our way back to the flat, around noon, planning to eat some of the food straightaway because we were both starving. 'Ouch,' I grumbled, in the lift, putting the carrier bags down and inspecting my hands. 'Why do they make those bags so they saw through your fingers when you're carrying them?'

And then we got to the door. We dropped the bags down and stood still. The little keyhole was blocked up and there was a metal bar nailed across the whole front door. Zoe thumped a fist on the door and swore. 'I don't believe this.'

I looked at her. 'What are we going to do?'

'We have to get in, somehow,' Zoe said, twisting at the padlock. 'A whole bunch of people will be here for the party in a few hours. I can't turn them all away. It'd be mortifying.'

'But how on earth will we get through all that?'

We heard some footsteps making their way up the stairs and turned, half-expecting to see the police or some council rents man. In fact, it was Dave. 'Ah,' he said, with his stupid grin. 'You've seen it. You're locked out, girls.'

'Thanks for that,' I said, nodding toward the padlock. 'We couldn't tell.' I could have kicked him.

'How did you know?' Zoe said. 'Did you see them doing it? Couldn't you have stopped them?'

'I've got a mate in the council works department,' Dave said. 'They had a tip-off that someone was squatting in here and they were sent round to make it secure. Nothing I could do about it, gorgeous.'

I swallowed, to stop myself telling Dave how disgusting I thought he was. But Zoe took a step towards him. 'Dave,' she said, in pleading sort of a tone. 'We're supposed to be having a party tonight. And anyway, all my stuff's in there – clothes and everything.'

'Have they cleared it out?' I asked.

Dave shook his head. 'Usually they would, but there's no point – the flats are being bulldozed in a few weeks' time. They were sure anyone in there was squatting and not meant to be there, so all they had to do was lock it up. No need to worry about any stuff in there – that's the squatters' problem. Oh – and there mightn't be any power. Or water. They'll probably have switched them off.'

Zoe sighed. Then she smiled at him. 'I bet you could get in. And get things back up and running, like you did before.'

Dave laughed and shook his head.

'Please,' Zoe said.

Dave took a step closer to her. 'Why would it be worth my time?'

Zoe put her head on one side and blinked at him. 'I'd be really grateful.'

I dug her in the back.

Dave went down to his own place and a few minutes later he was back with a bag of tools. 'You girls will get me into trouble,' he said, with a leery smile. While he crowbarred the metal bar on the door, Zoe pulled me aside.

'There's only one person who's spiteful enough to grass us up to the council,' she said. 'This is Kerry's work, I bet you.'

'You can't be sure,' I said. 'It could be someone else in the flats who's seen us going in and out.'

Zoe spread out her hands. 'Like who? This whole top floor is empty. And there are only a handful of other flats in the whole block that still have people in them. And we don't do any harm. We're not noisy or anything. No one here cares about us. There's only one person who's bothered. Because she's jealous.'

I closed my eyes. 'But you can't be certain.'

'Yes, I can. This is too much, Anna. I'm going to get her back.'

With a deep cracking sound, Dave pulled the metal bar off the door and then used another tool like a big flat screwdriver to force it open. 'There you go,' he said, pushing it wide, splinters of wood falling onto the floor. 'Door's not safe now, though. Don't leave anything valuable in here.' He winked at Zoe and gave her a nudge. 'I'll expect a thank-you sometime soon.' Zoe gave him another fake smile and I forced myself to do one too.

We were lucky – the power and water were still connected, for now. We spent the afternoon preparing food and Zoe made a brilliant Halloween soundtrack. She came out with me when I went home to get changed.

'I don't want to leave the flat unlocked, but Mum's pestering me on the phone,' she grumbled. 'I won't stay long. Just make sure you're back at the flat by seven. People should start arriving by then.'

For some reason, I felt anxious. When Mum tried to give me my favourite cheese on toast, I couldn't face it.

'Please – try to eat something,' Mum asked. She put a hand on my shoulder. 'I'm not stupid, Anna. I was fifteen once, and it doesn't even feel all that long ago. If you're going to a party I expect there'll be drink. I'd like to tell you not to touch it, but I know what I was like when I was your age, so there's no point in saying that. But you could at least try to be safe.'

'You're wrong,' I said. 'Well – I'm not saying I've never had alcohol. But I just don't really like it.'

'Good.' Mum looked me up and down. 'But you're so thin these days, too. It feels like you hardly touch your food. It's starting to frighten me, along with all the sleep problems.'

She was right, of course. Food was something I only picked at, these days. I knew my clothes were looser. 'There's nothing to worry about,' I promised her. 'And I need to go. I said I'd meet Zoe at seven. Don't stay up.'

At the door of the flat, Zoe looked so beautiful, all in black with a spiderweb top that she'd made herself, based on the one in the shop, and black ribbons plaited through her hair. But she was as white as the moon and a coldness came off her, as if I was standing next to an open freezer.

'Everything all right?' I asked. 'Your mum OK?'

I noticed she was trembling. I gave her a hug. 'Hey. What is it?'

'Nothing. Nothing at all. I just... the whole day's been going wrong. I wanted this party to be so good. But...' I could still feel her shaking.

'What's happened?' I pulled back and looked into her face. 'Tell me.'

She shook her head. 'The flat getting locked up. Bloody Kerry. My mother, trying to get in my way.'

'Forget all that,' I urged her. 'We're here. You look stunning. The flat is perfect. We can put all that out of our heads for tonight and worry about it tomorrow. Let's just make this the best party ever.'

The door was pushed open and there were a handful of the goths who Zoe knew from Dead Bouquet, Jodie and some of her friends. Jodie clattered a bag full of bottles onto the kitchen bench. 'Don't tell anyone,' she said.

'Ta,' Zoe said. 'I won't.' She was faking a brightness and a lightness that only I knew was a lie.

Jodie unscrewed the top off a bottle and poured dark red wine into flimsy paper cups. 'I'm not stopping,' she said. 'I'm meeting Dave in the pub in a few minutes.'

Zoe raised a cup at me. 'Happy Halloween, sinister sister.'

I laughed, took a sip and winced. The stuff was awful. 'Happy Halloween, ghoul-friend.'

It was all going really well. People brought drink with them, we rigged up the music though some stolen speakers and everyone was dancing. I noticed, though, that Zoe kept glancing at her watch. At around eight-thirty, she said: 'Hold the fort. Keep being the perfect hostess, or should that be ghost-ess, ha ha. I've just got something I need to do.'

'What?'

'Don't ask. Just keep the party going. I won't be very long.' Zoe wrapped her long coat around herself and scuttled out of the door towards the lift. I watched from the doorway as she pressed the button a few times and then, losing patience, started hurrying down the stairs.

The lift door opened and a few more people came out. I pointed them towards the flat, then stepped in and pressed the button for the ground floor.

Outside, I could see Zoe striding along the street. I followed, keeping as many paces behind as I safely could without losing sight of her. She went into The Cut. I lingered for a minute or two at the entrance where a street light flickered, threatening to go off. Then I crept after her into the muddy lane.

It was black as a grave, with the usual smells of mud and dog. I could hear voices. One of them was Zoe and the other one was Kerry. I stood still and listened.

'Tell the truth,' Zoe was saying. 'You grassed us up. Admit it.'

Kerry made some kind of a whimpering noise and I couldn't quite make out her words.

'Know what, Kerry? I'm in a whole load of trouble already. So much trouble that I don't care what I do next. Hurting you would be the best thing I've done all day, if you want to know.'

Kerry let out a loud sob. Zoe hissed at her. 'Make a great big row like that again and I'll make you really, really sorry.'

I was shivering hard. Part of me felt like turning and running back to the party. No – if I'm honest, I felt like running back home. I took a couple of silent steps forward.

I could see the dark shape of Zoe, with her back to me, shadowy shapes circling around her. And there, next to her, kneeling on the damp ground, was Kerry, wearing a light-coloured padded jacket, crying and cowering. In the darkness, it took me a minute to understand why. But then I saw it. Zoe was holding a knife to Kerry's neck.

I was about to shout out at them but then I froze. If Zoe got a shock, she might hurt Kerry badly, even by accident. I stayed still, barely even breathing, my head and body light, as if none of it was real.

'Thing is,' Zoe was saying. 'That flat was all I had. It was the safest place I could be. You know nothing about my life.'

Kerry let out another loud, wordless sob.

'Maybe it was breaking the law to stay in that flat. But I wasn't doing anyone any harm. And I was away from my mother. Remember those bruises you kept bleating on about? My mum did that. She does it whenever she needs to take her moods out on me. So sometimes I stayed in an empty flat that no one else wanted and no one got hurt. Especially not me.'

'S-s-sorry,' Kerry whimpered.

'You make out you're this sweet innocent kid who goes to church and wouldn't harm a fly. But you're full of spite. You wanted to see me in trouble, didn't you?'

Kerry moaned and shook her head.

'Yeah, you did. Just like when you tried to get me in trouble at home. Bet you thought you could have Anna to yourself, but that would never happen. She hates you just as much as I do. She'll never be your friend, not really. She only puts up with you 'cause she's too nice to tell you what she really thinks.'

I couldn't stand it any longer. 'Zoe,' I said. Just quietly. She turned her head towards me, but kept the knife pointing at Kerry. The dark, shapeless figures shimmered and I tried not to look at them, to fix my gaze on Zoe. Kerry's eyes were huge and swollen. 'Come on,' I said. I held out my hands to her. 'Leave Kerry alone.'

Zoe didn't move. Her hand trembled. 'Go away, Anna. I don't want you being part of this.' The shapes were flanking her, either side. I wasn't sure I could get near her – get past them.

'You – you're missing the party,' I said, still with my hands stretched out to her. 'It's going really well. Come back.'

'Kerry needs to learn what it feels like to be frightened,' said Zoe. 'She needs to know how I feel at home. And why causing trouble for other people is wrong. Just as wrong as anything I've ever done. I might pinch the odd thing from a big fat supermarket chain and I might stay somewhere without paying the rent. But I don't hurt anyone else.'

'You're hurting Kerry, right now,' I said. I could sense my own blood pulsing through my body, so hard and fast it felt like I might explode. 'You've told her what you think. She's not worth ruining your life for. Leave her alone.'

I took a few more steps towards her, still with my hands held out, feeling the sickening cold of the shadows enveloping her. 'Come back and – and – let's celebrate properly.'

Zoe locked eyes with me for a moment. Then she turned back to Kerry and lowered the knife. 'Another time,' she said. 'Watch your back. I won't forget.' And she tucked the knife into her coat and walked towards me. The blacknesses fluttered over Kerry, who was still huddled on the ground.

Zoe and I walked slowly back to the flats without saying a word. I glanced behind from time to time, but we weren't followed. I steered her into the lift, gently rubbing her arms to try to warm her up. We shuddered up to the top storey and stepped out to a blast of music and noise. Zoe wiped at her eyes and made straight for the kitchen, where she picked up a bottle of wine and tipped it up into her mouth.

'Don't,' I said. 'That won't help.' I pushed a plate at her. 'Have something to eat.'

'You have something to eat, Anna-rexic,' she spat at me.

I took a step back. 'Look,' I said, pointing towards the next room. 'This is a great party. This is your party and all these people are here because of you. Let's not fight.'

For a few seconds, Zoe looked around, anywhere but at me, her lips tight and her arms wrapped around herself. Then she breathed out. 'Sorry,' she whispered. 'Sorry.'

Someone tapped Zoe on the shoulder. It was a boy who I'd seen hanging around Dead Bouquet. I think he was a bit younger than Zoe, but he definitely had a crush on her. She turned and smiled at him, her teeth a little darkened by the wine. 'Hey,' she said, and grabbed him by the hand. 'Come and dance with me.'

I stood in the kitchen doorway and watched as Zoe led him into the middle of the floor and started to dance. A dark angel, surrounded by sadness and shadows and cold.

Then I turned away and left to go home. My life was about to implode.

21

The Misper

It was the early hours of the morning – 1st of November – when Mum and I were woken up by a loud hammering at the door. I stayed at the top of the stairs as Mum ran down to answer it, wrapping her dressing gown around her. I heard a man's voice announce it was the police and after a short conversation with them, Mum called me down.

The police officers were standing in our little hallway, rain on their jackets and caps. 'Anna, one of your friends has gone missing,' Mum said. 'The police want to ask you something.'

'Zoe?' I said, shivering in my pyjamas, my skin starting to prickle.

'Kerry Jones,' one of the officers said.

'Kerry?' I didn't expect that.

'Kerry left home to meet some friends at around half-past eight last night,' the officer said. 'But she never came home. We're sure she's fine, but need to find out where she went. Any ideas?'

Dumbly, I shook my head.

I sat in the bedroom most of the day watching out of the window, but I kept myself out of sight behind the curtain. My texts to Zoe had no answer. I kept hoping to see Kerry strolling back up the road like nothing had happened. But she didn't. There'd been at least one police car outside her house all day, sometimes other cars too. Police officers and people who looked like police, but without a uniform, in and out of the gate. Usually it was Kerry's dad who was opening and closing their front door, but just once it was Luke. I thought about giving him a quick wave, but I realised that actually, I didn't want him to see me. I'm not sure why. Also, the police were taking things out of Kerry's house, in bags. I took deep breaths to try to slow my thumping heart.

Mid-afternoon, there was another loud knock at our door. Two police officers, not in uniform. A fair-haired woman and a fat guy, wanting to talk to me. We went into the kitchen, sat around the table, and they told my mum she'd have to stay with me while they asked me questions.

'Where did you think I would go?' she said. She parked herself in a chair next to me and caught hold of my hand. There was a time, and it wasn't even all that far back, when just my mum being in the same room meant that nothing could possibly hurt me. I wondered when that changed. When she lost that power.

The fat guy was Rob Somebody and the woman, who was a bit nicer, was a sergeant, I think, and her name was Sandra Something. I couldn't always take in what they were saying and the weird thing was that I knew this even as they were talking to me, like they were speaking in Dutch or like something was blocking my ears. They went over and over the last time I'd seen Kerry. At first, I tried to make out I couldn't remember. But I couldn't keep it up.

So I admitted we'd seen her in The Cut around half-past eight on Halloween night.

'Where did you go after that?'

'To a party,' I said, avoiding Mum's eyes, but sensing her looking at me with a question on her face. I was going to have to own up about the non-existent Emma Wood.

'With Zoe Sawyer?'

I nodded.

'But Kerry didn't come with you? Why not?'

I bit my lip. 'It was a Halloween party. Kerry's church doesn't like her doing that sort of thing.'

'You don't know where she went?' Sandra asked. 'You sure about that?'

I shrugged, not meeting anyone's eye. 'I just thought she went home, that's all.'

They asked me about Kerry's other friends and I had to say she didn't have any. She really didn't. Just me and Zoe. No, in fact, just me, and I'm not very good at it, was what I didn't say.

Fat-Cop was scribbling stuff down all the time. My mum squeezed my hand. The little squeeze somehow made tears prick at my eyes.

Sandra Nice-Cop flicked at her notebook. Then she said: 'Tell me about Luke Jones.'

I could feel myself blushing. 'What about him?'

'He's Kerry's older brother. He's, what, seventeen? And he's your boyfriend, right?'

I glanced at Mum and back down at the table. 'Sort of.'

Sandra raised her pale eyebrows. 'Sort of? He says he is your boyfriend. He says you started going out together back in the summer.'

I nodded. 'Something like that.'

'He's a step-brother, isn't he? What sort of a relationship does he have with Kerry?'

I frowned. 'What do you mean?'

Sandra smiled at me. 'Do they get on?'

'Yes. Yes. He – he tries to look after her. She – he – he's great with her.'

Sandra flicked a page in her notebook. 'Perhaps you can help me with something else.'

I nodded, saying nothing.

'Does Kerry have a mobile?'

'Umm…' I thought about how to answer.

'Only her mum says she doesn't have one. But her brother texts someone called Kerry quite often. He's been texting all day asking where she is and if she's okay. A bit odd, don't you think?'

I breathed out, hard. 'I'm not sure.'

Sandra looked at me steadily. 'You would know, if Kerry had a mobile, wouldn't you? I know what you girls are like – never off their phones. But that number Luke's texting – it's also registered to him. So it could be that Luke's pretending to text his sister, to cover up for something. See what I mean?'

Heat rose up my neck and face. 'She does have a mobile,' I mumbled.

Sandra sat forward. 'She does? You're sure?'

'Yeah. It's Luke's old phone. He gave it to Kerry so she could message him if… if…'

'If?' Sandra prompted me.

'Like, if some of the girls at school were after her.'

'Does she get bullied a lot?'

'Sometimes.' I stared down at my hands. 'Once she got beaten up, in The Cut. It was a few months ago. Luke gave her the phone after that. She really only used it with him. Her mum doesn't know.'

I looked at the coppers and tried to work out what their faces were saying. They were like blank screens.

'He was just looking after her, like I said. He tries to keep her out of trouble. Including with her mother.'

My mum chipped in. 'Are you nowhere near finding the poor girl, officers?' She was still clutching my hand, a bit harder now. 'What do you think has happened?'

Sandra shook her head. Like she was going to tell my mum whatever she was thinking. 'We just don't know right now, Mrs Ellis, but we have some leads to follow. It's very possible she's quite safe, somewhere. But the problem for us is that the family didn't report her missing until quite late. That means if someone has taken Kerry, they could have gone a long way by now.'

She gave me a one of those smiles where people just move their lips and crinkle their face up, but it's not a real smile because their eyes don't flicker. 'If you think of anything else, Anna. Anything at all.' And she put a card with her telephone number on it down on the table.

November 2

Twenty-four hours later, there was still no sign of Kerry. I'd told the police what I knew. Well, some of it, anyway. I wasn't about to get Zoe into any more trouble. She still wasn't answering her phone and my mum wouldn't let me out of her sight, so I couldn't call at the flat. My dad called at her house, but he said there was no one there – it was all in darkness. I had no way of knowing whether the police had got to her. I just told them that we'd seen Kerry at The Cut and we'd left her to make her way home.

It wasn't quite all the facts of the matter. I left out a lot of stuff about the flats and whose party it was, because I reckoned all that didn't really matter. Except to get us into trouble – and maybe Jodie too, if they found out who let us into the flat in the first place. We were squatting and using illegal electricity and the place was kitted out with stolen stuff. And what if they found Zoe's knife? We could actually end up in some sort of prison.

The thing was, at first I didn't really think Kerry would stay missing. I didn't imagine she was in any kind of proper danger. I just expected that she'd soon come wandering back home, with some kind of a sob-story.

I texted Luke: *Any news x*. He texted back: *0. Can't talk now*. He didn't return the *x*.

The coppers came back twice that day. The second time, they asked me questions for more than an hour. Mum sat alongside me all the time. The police asked me quite a bit about the empty flat, because by now Luke had told them everything about it and thought she might've gone there. But she hadn't.

Before the officers left, I asked them if they'd spoken to Zoe.

'We can't say,' Sandra said, as she marched out of the door.

I texted again, for the hundredth time. *Zoe, where r u? Pls call. x*.

After the coppers left, I tried texting Luke again but I didn't get a reply. I called his number. His voice, when he answered, sounded heavy and flat.

'Are you OK?' I asked, knowing as the words came out that this was one of the dumbest things I've ever said.

He was silent for a few seconds. 'Not really.'

'I'm sorry,' I said. 'That must've sounded so stupid.'

More silence. Then Luke said: 'Do you know anything? Do you know where she went?'

'I promise I don't,' I told him. 'If I did, I wouldn't keep it to myself.'

'Not even to protect Zoe?'

'No, of course not.' I leaned against my bedroom wall, bile in my throat. 'I just want Kerry to come back safe.'

'They keep calling her the Mis-per,' Luke said, sounding suddenly furious.

'What's a Misper?'

'It's short for missing person. Like she's not real, she's just a ...project. A job. I keep saying, call her Kerry. Her name is Kerry.'

I didn't know how to reply to that.

'They've been searching our house. They've been in every room and every cupboard and up in the loft. They think we've done something to her.'

'Is that why they keep taking stuff from your house?'

Luke sniffed. 'They just say it's routine. That's their answer to every question – routine. But what they really mean is, they think we've hurt our Kerry. How could they think that, Anna?' It sounded like Luke was crying. Actually crying. I felt like a big stupid lump of uselessness. And guilt.

November 3

Monday. And still no Kerry. Almost everyone at school knew she was missing, because it had been on the local TV news and the ones that didn't soon found out, because the police came into assembly and said anyone who could help their enquiries should get in touch.

Some of the girls came up to me in the toilets, wanting to know all the details.

'She knows more than she's letting on,' one of them said. 'I can tell by her face.'

'And if that Zoe was involved,' another one of them started and they all agreed that Zoe would have had some hand in Kerry's disappearance. 'She was always picking on her.'

'You were *all* always picking on her,' I burst out and somehow, I found the nerve to walk through them towards the door. One of them pushed me hard so that I stumbled, but I kept walking.

The best parts of that day where when people left me alone. Even the teachers kept giving me that sad, sympathetic look and Mrs Bennett said if I wanted to talk about anything, I could always come to her. Like I would talk to a teacher.

And afterwards, when the police women said that Zoe was in hospital, I begged and begged them to tell me what had happened. Eventually Jenny said that when they'd gone to check out the flat, the day after the party, they'd found Zoe there, on her own. She'd taken some kind of pills and drink and they'd had to rush her to hospital. They'd known this all the time and hadn't bothered to tell me. I asked if

I could go and see her, but Jenny the Scarecrow shook her head.

'Not right now,' she said. 'Let's wait and see how she gets on, eh?'

'Her mum,' I blurted out. 'Have you spoken to Zoe's mum?'

Another silence. More loaded looks between Sandra and Jenny.

'She hits Zoe,' I said, before I could stop myself. 'She makes her life a misery. That's why Zoe's been staying at the flat. It's to get away from her.'

'Let's take you back home,' Sandra said. 'We need to ask you more questions about this, I'm afraid. The fact is – Zoe's mother is in hospital too. She has a head injury and we think Zoe may have had something to do with it.'

I heard myself moaning and clapped my hand to my mouth. Jenny's arm around my back kept me upright as I stumbled back along The Cut.

That evening, there were TV cameras in the street and journalists came knocking on the door. My mum told them to get lost. When a second set of reporters came around, she actually swore at them. Then she called Dad and he came over to sit with us.

Mum just left me alone, knowing I didn't want to talk right then, but my dad couldn't do that. He kept quizzing me about what had happened the night before and where the party was and what was this about my having a boyfriend?

'You're worse than the police,' Mum said to him. 'Leave the poor girl alone. She's in shock.'

'I'm sorry, Anna,' he said. He sat beside me on the sofa and put a big arm around my shoulders. I breathed in the smell of his suit, his aftershave. 'What do you want me to do?'

I couldn't find anything to say. I shook my head.

'Some people are out helping the police to search for Kerry,' he said. 'Do you want me to do that?'

'No, don't go away,' I pleaded. 'Just... just for now.'

We watched the local news. It showed Kerry's school photo and talked about what she was wearing the night before. Sandra the nice-cop was interviewed, but just for something like twenty seconds. It was long enough for her to say they were now concerned about Kerry's safety and that if anyone had any information – even if they didn't think it was important – they should call the police as soon as possible. Then they put a number up on the screen.

November 4

Still no Kerry.

Last night a programme called CrimeSeen filmed some sort of reconstruction of the last things Kerry did. Or, the last things they knew about. An actor girl who didn't look very much like Kerry at all was shown wearing the same chain-store jacket and waving goodbye to some out-of-shot friends in The Cut. So not how it happened at all. But it was supposed to make someone remember something. Something that would help find Kerry. It would be broadcast early next week, Sandra told us.

'You're not expecting to find her before then?' Dad asked.

Sandra didn't answer.

Mum let me stay away from school, because I couldn't eat or sleep. A doctor came and left some pills, but I wouldn't take them. I sat staring at the darkness outside, past my ghost-white reflection. In my head, I kept going over and over what happened on Halloween night. We left Kerry in The Cut, absolutely terrified. Why did I not just take her home? What made me think it was more important to look after Zoe? But I didn't even do that. I left the party when Zoe was in a half-dance, half-clinch with Goth Boy. And what happened after that? Did Kerry turn up? Did Zoe go back out to find her? Knots tightened and twisted in my insides when I thought how I dreaded Kerry turning up at my door and about all the times Zoe and I schemed to get rid of her. And now, I'd give just about anything to hear her knock.

Every now and then, the faint sound of squeals and muffled explosions cut through the heavy silence, as people set off early fireworks. I pressed my fist into my forehead and screwed up my eyes. I couldn't make sense of anything I'd done that night. Why did I leave the party so early – and what had Zoe done afterwards? She wasn't right that day – I knew it at the time. Why didn't I ask more questions?

Who did the police talk to about Kerry? Was it Dave and Jodie? Why should it be? What had they ever done but be kind to her? Kinder than Zoe and I were. I hoped the police wouldn't come back and ask me about them.

And why were the police taking things out of Kerry's house all the time?

There were so many questions. And no answers.

I don't know how long I sat there, not moving, staring out of the window as it grew darker and darker. I think at some point Mum must have come in and talked to me and put a blanket round my shoulders, because I can't remember how it got there. I talked to Zoe in my head and asked her all my questions, but I didn't get any response.

November 5

And still no Kerry.

Another visit from Jenny the Scarecrow and Sandra. I heard them murmuring to Mum and I saw their grim faces before she called me down to speak to them. They both gave me over-bright smiles.

It was becoming a routine. They told me to sit down; Mum made them both cups of tea; they asked how I was today. I asked how Zoe was. No change. And then they got to the point.

'We've gone through Zoe's phone,' Sandra said.

'And?' I thought I knew what was coming: that Zoe had asked Kerry to meet her that night in The Cut. But it was something else.

Jenny leaned forward. 'There was a message for you on it. Zoe texted you around three o'clock on Sunday morning. You never got that message, did you?'

I shook my head.

'No. It looked like Zoe saved it into her phone, but never sent it.'

I waited. 'And? What did it say?'

Sandra and Jenny flicked looks at each other and away again. Sandra coughed. 'Oh, look, here's your mum with that tea. You should have some, Anna. Put some sugar in it.'

I shook my head. 'What did the message say?'

'Sweet tea's good for shock.' Mum handed me a mug.

My fingers felt slippery as I grasped the handle. 'What did the message say?'

Jenny put her hand on my knee. I could smell her musky perfume and faintly, cigarette smoke. 'Zoe was in a very disturbed state of mind that night, wasn't she?'

I blew steam across the surface of the tea, took a sip and pursed my lips at the taste.

Jenny went on. 'We have pieced some things together. Zoe had a big row with her mum and it got violent. We understand Zoe pushed her mother and she fell, hitting her head hard. When Zoe left home, her mother was unconscious and bleeding.'

I nodded.

'Mrs Sawyer is going to be all right. That's the good news,' Sandra cut in.

'What did the message say?'

'Zoe thought her mum was … She thought she may be dead.'

The mug felt heavy and all my limbs felt light. I put the tea down on the table and clasped my hands together to stop them trembling. 'Zoe thought she'd killed her own mum?'

Jenny gave a little incline of her head. 'She did. She wrote a text to tell you. She saved it as a draft on her phone. And then she took some of her mother's tablets.'

Mum passed me a tissue and put a firm arm around my shoulder.

'The message said, *the magic's gone all bad*. What did she mean, do you think? Zoe says…' Sandra glanced down at her notebook. 'She says, *You were right. It's gone too far*. Do you know what she's talking about?'

I shook my head, slowly, side to side, my throat aching. Zoe had put it just right, though. The magic had all gone bad.

'Could I have…?' I hardly dared ask the question. I wiped my eyes and breathed out. 'If she'd sent the message…'

'Could you have saved her? We don't know. It might have helped if she'd got to the hospital quicker, I suppose,' Sandra started.

I heard Mum clear her throat.

'But the fact is, she didn't send the text, so there's no way you can take any responsibility for this, Anna,' Jenny said, her voice soft. She leaned forward and put a hand on mine. 'She's going to survive. She'll be all right, I promise, so you can stop worrying. But it'll take a long time and she won't be going back to live with her mum.'

I put my knuckle into my mouth and chewed at it. Mum's fingers tightened on my shoulder. It was late and I watched as one single, final, fantastic firework hissed past into the sky, leaving a lingering trail of silver sparks that floated in the air like the ghost of a bird's wings. And something about it made me catch my breath. 'Make them OK,' I said, to the empty air. 'Make them both OK. Please.'

November 6

Dad drove me to the hospital. Jenny insisted on coming in with me, to Zoe's little side room off a long corridor.

I've never seen anyone lie so still. If it wasn't for the little pulsing lights around her, she could've been a corpse.

I sat with her for a few minutes, stroking her hand, telling her I missed her, pleading with her to wake up. A nurse watched us and smiled at me. 'That'll do her good,' she said. 'Always talk as if she can hear you.'

'You know what you could do?' I said to the nurse. 'Play music to her. I can tell you what bands she likes.'

'Yes, please,' the nurse nodded. 'Anything to get a response.'

I rummaged in my bag and pulled out my phial of perfume from Dead Bouquet. I waved it under Zoe's nose. I swear her lashes flickered. But no one else saw.

I went back there the next day and the next, with speakers rigged up next to Zoe's bed and some incense sticks from Dead Bouquet. The nurse refused to let me light them, though, no matter how much I argued with her. I ended up dropping some perfume onto a tissue and tucking it into the sheet. The scent of another of Zoe's favourites, Something Wicked, drifted into the sterile air of the hospital room.

I didn't know what to do, exactly. The nurse said to keep talking to her, but I kept running out of things to say, so sometimes I just sang along to the tracks, so she would know I was still there, stroking her hand, thinking how much she'd hate to see how chipped her nail polish was. The singing helped me not to think too hard. I tried not to focus on those dark shadows that loomed over the head of her bed, the grey-black, cloudlike presences that I could

231

only ever see if I didn't look straight at them. Zoe needed me, so they weren't going to scare me away.

I'd been there around three hours when I felt a tiny movement under my fingers and I jumped, as if a little flame had been lit. Zoe's hand trembled.

'Zoe,' I whispered, glancing backwards to see if any of the medical staff were around. 'Wake up. It's me. It's Anna.'

For a long few seconds, nothing. And then Zoe jolted, as if she'd been struck by lightning, opened her eyes wide and started to cough. She tugged at the mouthpiece helping her breathe and pulled it out. She stared at me, still coughing, then swore in a sort of a splutter.

'It's all right. It's all right. You're awake,' I gabbled, trying really hard not to cry. 'I should get a nurse.'

'Wait.' Zoe tried to sit up, then let her head fall back onto the ice-white of the hospital pillowcase. 'Don't go. Anna, there's… there's something…'

'She's okay. Your mum,' I blurted out, because I guessed that was the first thing she'd be worrying about.

Zoe closed her eyes and sighed. 'Thanks. I thought…'

'I know. You should've told me, though.'

She chewed her dry lip. 'I was so scared. I'm sorry. Are you sure she's all right? You're not just saying it to make me feel better?'

'No, of course not. But –'

Zoe half-sat up again. 'Hey. Hold my hands. There's something I want to say.'

I hesitated. I should tell her about Kerry. Could Zoe cope with the news that Kerry was missing? She looked so thin, like a bare winter twig.

Zoe gave both my hands a weak squeeze. 'The magic,' she began.

I shook my head. 'Let's not talk about that. It's over. We shouldn't have…'

'No. I shouldn't have.' Zoe's soft voice dropped to a whisper and I leaned in a little closer. 'What I worked out, on Halloween night, was that you're the one. The one with the power.'

'I don't know what you mean. I think it was maybe all just, you know – coincidence. Things that would've happened anyway.'

Zoe closed her eyes. 'It was more than that and you know it. It went bad for me and I know why. I wanted the wrong things. I turned it all against people and it came right back at me.' Zoe's breathing was fast and shallow. 'But you – you always tried to do the right thing. And that's when it worked best.'

I shrugged.

Zoe grasped my hands a little harder. There was a heat between our fingers. 'You've got something special. Me – I was just playing at it. But you have something more than that. I mean it. When we did our magic, all the real power came from you. You have…' she blinked a wetness away from her lashes. 'You have a good heart, I think. Not like me.'

I couldn't bear it. My throat ached as I tried to swallow back the urge to cry. 'Don't talk like that. Please.'

Zoe's head sank back and her eyes started to close. 'Come back tomorrow, yeah?'

'She's awake?' a voice bellowed. The nurse bustled up behind me and pressed a button to call for help. As a doctor rushed in, the nurse steered me out of the room. 'Well done,' she said. 'You brought her round. Good girl.'

The door closed and I was left there, my head ringing with Zoe's words. I started to text my dad, my fingers still tingling and trembling. If I'm so powerful, I thought, how come I have never felt so helpless in all my life?

22

A good heart

I couldn't get Zoe's words out of my head. She'd turned around everything I ever thought about us. I wanted to do anything to please her, so she would always be my cool, funny, magical friend. But for her, I was the one with the power. And what she'd said about a good heart – that sort of echoed what my dad said about me, the time we argued. And what Kerry said, lots of times. And what Luke said, too. How come everyone thought I had this thing, this good heart, when all I felt was that it got me into trouble? I didn't understand it, but it felt, in a strange way, as if Zoe had handed me a heavy weight. I had to work out what to do with it.

Dad had brought Barney back for a while. I sat tugging at the dog's ears, the way he likes, breathing in his smell and taking comfort from his warm body. 'What would you do, if you knew you had power, eh, Barney? What would someone really powerful do, right now? Because I don't know.'

Barney shook my hands away, turned his big head and licked my face. I wiped it with the edge of my sleeve. 'That's no help, you daft dog. What I need to do is find Kerry. And somehow… I don't know…get rid of those shadows around Zoe. Something horrible's hanging around her. And me. You know it, don't you, because you won't go in my room. You see them, whatever they are. It's the same thing.' I sighed and pulled him closer, my heartbeat in time with his slow panting.

And then I stood up. Barney jumped up with me. 'Yep. We are going for a walk. Come on, boy.'

With Barney on the lead, making me feel safe, I walked the long way around to the high rises, avoiding The Cut. It was dark already and damp, with that smell November has, of everything dying. I stared up at the block of flats, looming over Scrogg's Field. 'I hate this place,' I whispered to Barney. 'I wish I'd never seen it.'

I'd tried to put Dave and Jodie out of my mind. I didn't want to put my and Zoe's troubles on to them. Plus, they were out, weren't they, on Halloween night, so probably, they had nothing to do with whatever happened to Kerry. But I reckoned someone with a strong heart and mind would ask the question, just to make sure. Barney padded up the steps with me to the ninth floor and sat on my foot as I knocked at Jodie's door.

It took a few minutes for her to answer. I'd been about to turn away when I heard her footsteps and the lock click.

'Oh. It's you,' she said and sniffed, turning away, but leaving the door open. I followed her inside.

'You okay?' I asked. She was wearing her dressing gown and slippers. There was a row of used mugs on the table and a pile of empty cigarette boxes. 'Are you poorly?'

Jodie shrugged and flopped onto a chair. She had no make-up on and looked even more grey-faced than usual. 'What d'you want?'

'You've heard about Kerry?'

Jodie flashed a glare at me. 'It's not my fault. Stupid kid.'

'I didn't say –' I paused and stared back at her. I got the clear sense she knew something, unless we were talking about two different things. 'You know her parents are frantic? The police are looking for her.'

'I don't know where they are,' Jodie snapped, reaching for a fresh packet of cigarettes and a lighter.

'I just wondered if you'd seen… hang on, what do you mean, they?' I waited as Jodie flicked and clicked at her lighter, waiting for a spark. My heartbeat started to speed up.

Jodie sucked for a long moment on the cigarette and took even longer to blow out a stream of grey smoke. 'It's not the first time he's done it. Run off with someone else. He'll be back.'

I pulled a fidgeting Barney closer to me and pushed him into a sitting position. I swallowed hard to get some moisture back into my mouth. 'Dave? Are you saying that Kerry… and Dave…?'

Jodie picked up a piece of notepaper from amid the half-drunk coffee cups and the ashtrays. She threw it across the table at me. I unfolded it to see Kerry's babyish, untidy handwriting.

Dear Jodie, Kerry wrote. *Dave said not to say anything but I feel bad because you have always been kind to me. We are going away together. I am sorry if you are hurt. But I love him and I want to get away from here because I'm scared and he says he will look after me. Love from Kerry.*

'Stupid kid,' Jodie muttered again, staring past me.

My words wouldn't come out and I found myself opening and closing my mouth like a puppet. 'When did you get this? How long have you known?'

She shrugged with one shoulder, like a sulky toddler. For a second, I wanted to slap her. 'A few days,' she said, after a silence. 'I was nice to that kid. Felt sorry for her. And look what she did in return.'

'The police...' I said, still struggling to find the right thing to say. 'Her mum...'

'I can't help the police. I don't actually know where they are. Dave's a builder. He works all over the country. What am I supposed to do, anyway? Tell the police that my boyfriend's run off with a schoolkid? How do you think that makes me feel?'

I stood up and Barney loyally leapt up with me. 'Well,' I said. 'That's what I'm going to do.' I started for the door, stopped and turned back. 'You know what? You were always telling Zoe and me to grow up and look after Kerry. And you're prepared to let her family go out of their minds and the police run around like idiots, while you sit on this –' I waved Kerry's note at her – 'just because you're feeling sorry for yourself.'

Jodie glared back at me. Then her pale face went pink and crumpled into a sob.

For a second, I wanted to put my arms around her. But it would have to wait. 'I'm sorry,' I said, stuffing the note in my pocket. 'It's horrible. Dave's evil and yeah, Kerry's been stupid. But you should've said something.'

'Anna!' Jodie wailed after me. 'Don't! It's too late! The police might arrest me!'

I kept walking.

'It was that Zoe she was really scared of. That's why she's done it,' Jodie shouted. 'So you're to blame too, Saint Anna! Remember that!'

I pushed Barney out of the door and slammed it, hard, behind me. Then we ran all the way down nine flights of stairs, the sounds of Jodie's screaming in my ears.

We were still running when we reached the end of my street and my head was buzzing so much I didn't notice Luke until he was right in front of me. 'Hey,' he said, holding out his arm as if he was flagging down a bus. 'Anna. You OK? What's up?'

I stopped and gulped in the cold air. It hurt the back of my throat and made my eyes water. 'Kerry,' I gasped. 'I... I know something.'

Luke grabbed my wrists. 'What? What do you know?'

I blurted out what I could, with Luke shaking his head and swearing. 'So I...' I panted, still breathless. 'I'm taking this note to the police.'

'Go on, then.' Luke stepped backwards, away from me. 'Better late than never, I suppose.'

'What do you mean? I've only just –'

'You must've known something. Or you might've guessed. How could you, Anna? Why did you let Kerry get involved with a creep like that? No – don't say anything. I know the answer. Because Zoe is all you're bothered about. Protecting Zoe and her weird friends, making sure Zoe's OK.'

Luke spun around and strode away, shouting back at me over his shoulder. 'Go and tell the police, then. Though it's probably too late.'

I couldn't move. Barney whimpered up at me and so, trembling so hard his lead made rattling noises, I made myself walk on. It's funny, I thought, wiping my eyes. Everyone tells me I have this good heart. Everyone seems to admire it. Except for Luke. And he's the only one I gave it to.

The next morning, at the hospital, Zoe was dressed and sitting in a chair next to her bed, a cardboard box at her feet.

I gave her a hug. She smelled odd, of some sort of hospital soap. I nodded towards the box. 'What's that?'

'All my worldly goods.' Zoe leaned down and pulled out a couple of magic books. 'All the stuff that wasn't nicked and the only clothes worth keeping.' She held out the books to me. 'Here. I want you to have these.'

I was about to say no, when the thought came to me that it was more important to be kind to Zoe right now than to argue about the rights and wrongs of witchcraft. 'Thanks,' I said. 'But why?'

'I'm being sent into exile.' Zoe gave me a thin smile. 'Some sort of clinic. Madhouse, they mean. About as gothic as you can get, though, right?'

'A clinic? But…' I picked up a leaflet from the bedside table for something called The Cloisters. 'You mean you really won't be going home?'

'My mum's not fit to look after me. And I'm not fit to be with her. Win-win, eh?' Zoe was still trying to fix a sort of a smile onto her face.

A woman wearing a blue, medical-looking trouser suit came in. 'Ready, Zoe? Had a chance to say goodbye to your friend? We should get going. We've a long drive.'

'It's at the other end of the country,' Zoe said. She held open her arms and I fell into them, holding her as tight as I could.

'I don't want you to go.'

'Don't make me cry,' Zoe said, with a sniff.

'I'll message you.'

'No phone.' Zoe's voice sounded cloudy.

'I'll write you letters, then. Or something. I promise.'

Zoe nodded. 'Thanks, Anna.'

The uniformed woman gently prised us apart and took Zoe by the arm, steering her towards the door.

'It's not forever,' I said, picking up the box and handing it to Zoe. 'And when you leave this – this clinic place – what then?'

'Who can say?' Zoe gave a tiny shrug. 'It'll be… like the magic books say. A world of infinite possibilities.'

23

Chasing shadows

Back at home, I leafed through Zoe's books. The pages still smelled of incense and I held them close to my face, breathing them in. Mum said she wished I would just put them away, but I couldn't. It wasn't just that they felt like my last link to Zoe. The pages seemed to be whispering to me. We had unfinished business.

I waited till Mum was out at work and then I tried to get Barney to come up the stairs with me, but as usual he stopped at the landing and set up a growl. 'I could do with you beside me, boy,' I said, tucking the book under my arm so I could stroke him. 'But I won't make you. Just sit there, OK?'

Barney sat, with a throaty whine. I patted his head and put my hand on the door. Barney whimpered again, louder, and a chill went through my whole body. But I turned the handle and pushed the door open.

I dropped the things I'd brought with me on to the bed. It was darker than it should be and it felt more than silent. It was as if something was holding its breath, listening to the thudding of my heart. Waiting to see what I would do.

I placed white candles in the four corners of the room and lit them, shushing Barney as he fussed outside. In my incense burner, I put ground basil from the kitchen and some drops of a scent from Dead Bouquet, called

MyrrhMyrrh. It was the closest I could get to the book's suggestions for psychic cleansing and protection.

Next was the hardest bit. It was always Zoe who made up our spells and I felt like I was no good at it. She was so clever with words. Mine felt a bit silly. But I was going to have a try.

I kept my voice low, to disguise how shaky it sounded and I started to chant something from the witchcraft book, with a little extra line added in, telling the presence to leave. Barney interrupted with what sounded like a sort of loud, doggy sob. I could hear him shuffling and panting right outside the bedroom door, as if he couldn't decide whether to come in or not.

I waited. The candle flames juddered, though there were no draughts or open windows and the air felt still and heavy. I breathed in the scent of the basil and myrrh, hoping it would somehow help to have the fumes inside my head. Then I did the chant again, a little louder this time. The curtains fluttered and as I came to the end of my words, there was a sudden, violent swoosh as they pulled themselves open. I found myself staring, eyes wide and heart hammering, at my reflection in the night-black glass. The candle nearest to the window went out, leaving a ghostly trail of grey in the air. I whipped my head around as the next one went out. Then the third. And the fourth. I couldn't see a thing.

I took some deep, long breaths and wiped a moustache of sweat away from my upper lip. Something was happening. My whole body was shaking and I felt like I was standing on the edge of something deep and dark. But I had to keep going. Barney started scratching, frantically, at the bedroom door and his whine turned to a louder growl. For a second, my brain went back to normal: Mum was going to go mad when she saw the paintwork. 'Shh. Calm down, boy. Sit!' I hissed at him.

I swallowed. One more time. The magic books were quite big on the rule of three. I stood up, my knees trembling, coughed and started again. I only got partway through the words this time, when the notepaper whisked out of my fingers and into the air. A breeze, out of nowhere and colder than death, whirled its way around the room, tugging at my hair and my limbs, knocking down books, my clock, my lamp, bringing them all crashing to the floor. There was a strong smell of earth and decay. I squeezed my eyes shut and crouched down, covering my head with my hands and yelling, 'Stop it! Get out of here! Leave Zoe and me alone! Whatever we did to bring you here, we're sorry! We don't want you anymore!'

The door burst open with a crash and Barney threw himself into the room, barking and snapping at the air. The window panes rattled, as if someone was trying to force them open. My posters ripped themselves from the walls and a photo in a frame clattered to the floor and smashed into pieces. I threw myself onto the bed and pulled the duvet over me, shaking so hard the bed hammered against the wall. Something heavy landed on top of me and I screamed, before realising it was Barney, trying his best to guard me. His barks were like gunfire, never letting up against the crashing and smashing of my room tearing itself apart.

I don't know how long it was before things went quiet. I waited, trembling, for a few seconds. Pulling down the edge of the duvet, I peered over it into the carnage that was my bedroom. Was it over? Breathing hard, I clambered across Barney and lowered my trembling legs to the floor. I reached up and snapped on the light, which shone for a beat. Then with a small explosion the bulb popped and the room was dark again – too black to make anything out, though the stench of decay was so thick I could almost touch it. Something small and hard hit me in the face and I yelped, trying to smack it away. And again and yet again –little pebbles, hard as bullets. I threw my hands up to my face, feeling grit on my skin, and doubled over in pain, attacked from all sides by stones and soil, filling my eyes, my hair, my fingers. I flung myself onto the floor, curling up tight in a ball. It was like being on a battlefield. I didn't know if I could survive. Barney's howl seared through my whole body as the stones and filth rained down. The thought flashed through my mind that I was going to be buried alive. And then, a mind-splitting crash as the window smashed open, letting in a gust of freezing night air. I stayed in a shivering heap on the floor, listening, chewing my knuckles to stop myself from screaming out loud. But everything had stopped. And there was a strange, empty silence.

I opened my eyes, blinking back my tears and peered around. The whole room smelled like a churchyard and the floor was covered in soil and the smashed remains of my things. But the air was dead and quiet again. The only sound was Barney's panting. He shuffled over to me and thrust a wet nose into my face. I pushed myself up with my hands. There was the sound of sobbing, turning into a wail. The howling came from me.

24

Starting again

There isn't much I can tell you about the weeks afterwards, because they're something of a blur. I remember Mum coming back and finding me, weeping and shivering in my room, with Barney steadfastly by my side. Then there were doctors, sleeping pills, counselling sessions. So many people suggested I'd smashed up my room all by myself that even I started to wonder how much had all been in my own head.

Sandra came to see me and told me I was brave and wonderful, though I couldn't have felt any less like it. The police put out pictures of Dave alongside those of Kerry. And from time to time, there'd be new reports: someone looking like Dave or Kerry had been spotted, in Southheads, in Fellingstall, or even further away. But they never came to anything. I guess her family never stopped looking for her, though Luke and I never spoke to each other again.

Dad moved back in with Ellie and shortly afterwards he told us that she was going to have a baby. He said it was good news. Something to celebrate, after all the Kerry stuff – and that if I wanted, Barney could come to live with us for good. I packed him into the car: my consolation prize. But also my bodyguard.

In my head, I would talk to Zoe and I would be furious with her for not being around, because she was the only one who would've understood how I felt right then. And then I would say sorry. I was only angry with her for leaving me and not replying to any of my letters to The Cloisters, for not letting me know if I'd chased away those cold shadows that followed her around even more than they did with me. It felt like there were big, ice-blasted holes in my life where other people used to be.

In the street, people put their Christmas decorations up. Fairy lights blinked behind windows and on the rooftops, all except one house – Kerry's. I thought how this would be my first Christmas without Dad here and then I hated myself for being so selfish. After all, this would be the Jones's first Christmas without Kerry. Funny how days that are meant to be happy just get worse when you're missing someone. It made me wonder what they were all for.

First week in January, we moved house again. Mum said it wasn't doing me any good, passing Kerry's home every day and being so close to where everything happened. She began using the words 'fresh start'.

And this is it. I give a last salute to Mum and I walk in through the toughened glass doors, out of the rain. I follow the crowds of other kids until I get to a reception desk, and a soft-voiced secretary takes me along to my new classroom. The other kids stare at me as the teacher tells them my name. They know no one starts a new school just after Christmas unless something weird's happened. I'm just hoping no one links me with the name of Kerry, the girl from the other side of the city who went missing and never came back. The girl I wanted rid of so I could be with Zoe, who I lost in the end after all. Kerry, the girl who isn't following me around anymore and who will be with me for the rest of my life.

'Well,' says the teacher. 'We have two empty seats, so you have a choice, Anna.'

I scan the classroom. At the back, a girl with rainbow-coloured hair is staring through the window, as if in her head she's already somewhere out there. I wait for her to turn and notice me, but she doesn't so much as glance. In the second row, another girl is blushing, adjusting her glasses and throwing me an eager smile. I cross my fingers and say a few words in my head to Zoe.

Then I make a choice.

THE END

ACKNOWLEDGMENTS

The Misper was very loosely based on something that happened to me when I was a child. It was a quite insignificant incident in many ways and I promise it was not as dark as the fictional events in this novel! But it shows that strange and small things can inspire a story.

I'd like to thank Trevor Byrne for editorial input into a very early draft, which transformed it from a story for younger children into one targeted at teen readers. Huge thanks are also due to my agent, James Essinger, for his editorial work and his stubborn faith in the story.

Thanks, always, to Mark, Naomi, Patrick and Mary for their constant love and support. As ever, this book is for them.